Brenda

Hope you

like It.

Sylvia 2018

Notable

Quotable

A Gemstone Novel

June 2018

Notable Quotable

By

Sylvia Louise Alexandria Lacey

Notable
Quotable

My collection of Quotes and Antidotes

Sylvia Louise Alexandria Lacey

Quotes have always been a hobby of mine; it began back in school, passing notes all the time. This was the way we all kept in touch, talking, sharing and gossiping too much. Recently I pulled down a box from a shelf; they made me laugh in-spite of myself. Jokes and quotes, cards and notes, they were all such funny antidotes.

High school, I became 'a working girl' a job in the city looked might pretty. My schedule was great; a few classes, some lunch, and then headed downtown, like the working bunch. One cold November day my father pasted away, it was a shock; it was a nightmare, what more can I say. My friends were amazing, with cards and kind words; they clung to me close, like sweet hummingbirds. I kept their old cards and notes from yesteryear, they were funny, they were friendly, and downright sincere.

So I was the girl who passed around notes and found myself with quite a collection of quotes. Looking back I was surprised by my naiveté, but maybe a bit more, even today. When Barak became President he was too much to bear, from false news, to fake news and that damn, Obama care. I used to watch the 'Today Show' and believed what they reported, and now I'm afraid they might all be deported. These morning shows should report on something worthwhile, before they all find themselves in exile.

Political quotes are all the rage, their snarky and funny and leave you half-dazed. President Trump maybe a thorn in some peoples side, but he's a man of God who won by a landslide. Please before anyone has something to say, America spoke their mind, on voting day. Oprah is someone who demands our respect, whining about White Privilege, and our new President. I'm sorry to say she thinks it's her job, when all she should do, is to answer to God. Also I discovered and it was no shock at all, that Malcolm X was a drug-addict and bi-sexual you all. His words created hate and strife, what a sad state, for such a young life. (Assassinated in 1965) At least Tupac had something to say, he was a product of his environment, when he passed away. (Assassinated in 1996)

MLK (Assassinated in 1968), was no different than JFK (assassinated 1963) two men in the 60's with plenty to say. Both were playboys so carefree and gay, with women and innuendo that plagued them each day. These men were politicians, both in their prime, but JFK never hid behind God, he was just a bootleggers-son, who *fucked'em* two at a time.

So you will not see any quotes from them in here, you will however read quotes, from dear old Shakespeare. This book is a collection of words, quotes and praises, about faith and hope in beautiful phrases. There is one thing that I must address, why remove God and cause all this stress? Our streets are unsafe a hovel for sin, because when you take God out of your neighborhoods—the DEVIL moves in.

I also included quotes on life and death, because so many have taken, their final breath. The controversy over gun-control is getting pretty old. To remove Arms from law abiding citizens is just way too bold. Guns still find their way in the hands of the corrupt, that is something my friends, we must interrupt.

On a more positive note I'd just like to say, I'm moving forward with each passing day. The family has weathered many hard times, but we Lacey's survive, like fine old red wine.

I hope you enjoy this quirky little book, and I thank you God for showing me your work. I thank my family for their love and insight, and hope to see you all, on Family Dinner Night (_)3.

Notable Quotable

Table of Contents

Chapter 1 Quotes from Friends

Whether you are hear or yonder, whether you remain or wander, that's why friends grow fonder. Whether you are all alone, or just want to remain unknown, a friend is no further than your phone. Friends are like cocktails, some salty, some sweet, but when the liquor is popping, some fall at your feet. Don't let the blues get in your way; remember my friends, I'm just a couple of blocks away. Friends have the antidotes like perfect equations; they're witty and smart on any occasion. Now family is different, they show-up on the scene, their loud, their family, you know what I mean. They comfort you always with tender loving care; they even make sure, you don't vomit in your hair. This chapter is filled with words from my friends; some are hysterical, right down to the end. Family is different they joke and they fuss, but only about things that are funny to us. Family and Friends will always share more, whenever the laugher begins to pour.

****

"Most women have two assholes, one they sit on, the other they send to work." Alex Lacey

***

"Show me your friends and I'll show you your future." Tom Lacey

***

"A joyful life is an individual creation that cannot be copied from a recipe" Sam Ovens

***

"Don't tell me the sky's the limit when there are footprints on the moon." Evelyn Lacey

***

"Whether good or bad it's just an experience" Anne Dunne

***

"Man who stands on toilet—is high on POT." Terrie Walls

***

"Drive it like you stole it." Alex Lacey

***

"I have a head for business and a bod for sin." Melanie Griffith

***

"The United States has become a place where entertainers and professional athletes are mistaken for people of importance." Ken Darnall

***

"We can only blame ourselves for all the crime and violence today. We removed all the phone booths and now Superman has nowhere to change." Caroline Sierra Vereline

***

"Tough times never last—tough people do." George Anthony

***

"Have more than you show and speak less than you know." Tiffany Lacey

***

"There are 3 kinds of people, those who make things happen, those who watch things happen and those who say WHAT HAPPENED." Louie Lacey

***

"You'll only failure—if you don't try." Brenda Clark

***

"I'm not God I can't change your life." Laura

***

"Love means never having to say 'you're sorry.'" Love Story

***

"I adore pretty things and witty words." Kate Spade (suicide 6/2018)

***

"Never be afraid to try new things." Brenda Clark

***

"I'll love you forever; I'll like you for always as long as I'm living, my baby you be always." Rebecca Modock

***

"When life throws you lemons, make LEMONADE." Gwen Darnall

***

"Your momma is so stupid—she sold her car for gas money."

***

"Remember your Company was looking for a good person whey they hired you." George Anthony

***

"Worries don't matter, it's how you handle them that matters." Abriana Heinz

***

"Hate the game, not the player." Kenny Cotto

***

"Do good you get good, do bad, you get WORSE!" Erika Heinz

***

"Life is too short for a bad cigar, a bad scotch or a bad cup of coffee." Tony Anthony

***

"Didn't care yesterday, don't give a shit today, probably won't give a fuck tomorrow." TWOW

***

"Eat, drink and be Glad." Erika Heinz

***

"The same one who mistreated you will end up needing you."
Ice Cube

***

"Here today, here tomorrow, here today, gone tomorrow." A.
Kilbane

***

"Avoid posting your personal problems on social media. Your
personal problems require personal solutions, not social
attention." Kenny Cotto

***

"I'd rather shoot for perfect and MISS, than shoot for imperfect
and HIT." George Anthony

***

"If you're not having fun, you're not doing it right." Trish
Marotta

***

"So is a man think it. So is a man be it." George Anthony

***

"God only gives us what we can handle." Erika Heinz

***

"Flowers—poor people's jewelry," Karen Walker

***

"Same old shit, just a different day." Debbie Arington

***

"Life is a dance," Erika Heinz

***

"At the end of the day it's not what you do, it's how you do it!"
Chris B.

***

"My luck is like a bald guy who just won a comb." George C.

***

"If you think someone is staring at you, Yawn. If they yarn,
they were staring." Mom.

***

"I want to love you without clutching, appreciate you without
judging, join you without invading, invite you without
demanding, leave you without guilt, criticize you without
blaming, and help you without insulting. If I can have the same
from you—then we can truly meet and enrich each other."
Linda Barrier

***

"I'm emotionally constipated; I haven't given a shit in days."
Bar joke

***

"The good thing about water is you can drink it at work, the
best thing about Vodka, it looks like water." Dean Martin

***

"Sometimes you run into people who change your life for the better, those people are called bartenders." Raj

***

"A relationship is like the Taj Mahal. Everybody appreciates how beautiful it is, but no one understands how difficult it was to build" Sandeep Kumar

***

"Nothing lasts forever, so live it up, drink it down, laugh it off, avoid the drama, take chances and never have regrets. Because at one point everything you did was exactly what you wanted." Marilyn Monroe Rip 1962

***

"Stay away from 'Still' people. Still broke, still complaining, still hating and still nowhere." Sylvia Lacey

***

"Hurt an artist and you will see a masterpieces from what you have done." Arun Kumar

***

"When you're in a car accident, it either makes you never drive again, or makes you a better driver." Alex Lacey

***

"Only those who want everything done for them are bored." Mrs. Bessie Crossin

***

"The only person who can change your life is you." Favored by Debbie Arington

***

"Confession is an act of honesty and courage" Pope John Paul

***

"Only do what the heart tells you." Princess Diana

***

"Do not tell secrets to those whose faith and silence you haven't already tested." Queen Mother Elizabeth I

***

"Let us not take ourselves too seriously—none of us has a monopoly on wisdom"…Queen Elizabeth II

***

"90% of parenting is thinking—when you can lie down again." Grandma

***

"Everything is funny as long as it happens to someone else." Will Harper

***

"Some people are like clouds when they disappear it's a beautiful day," Mary Stone

***

"If you fall I'll be there—Floor." Amy Stone

***

"Auto correct can go straight to hell." Samantha

***

"I'm not insulting you I'm describing you." Amy Mather's

***

"With great power, comes great electricity bills," Ma

***

"I'm sorry did I roll my eyes out loud?" Lara

***

"Follow you heart, but take your brains too." Mrs. Washington

***

"A penny saved is a penny earned." Audrey Banks

***

"The harder you work, the luckier you get," Mavis

***

"I would go out of my mind, but I can't find the exit." Nancy

***

"When people asked me if Dean Martin drank, let me put it this way, if Dracula bit Dean in the neck, he would get a Bloody Mary." Red Buttons

***

"Do you pray before you eat—no we're Hungarian, my mom knows how to cook." Aunt Sylvie

***

"Twinkle, Twinkle little snitch, Mind your own business—you nosey bitch." Caroline Martin

***

"We're not your family—we're trouble." Tom Lacey

***

"Everyone has a friend during each stage of life, but only lucky ones have the same friend in all stages of life." Gwen Darnall

***

Chapter 2. For the Fun of it

A man attends Mass like a religious fanatic; down on his knees praying like an addict, 'Dear God, please help me win the lottery, I'm dead-broke and living, in scant-poverty. The bill collectors hound me each day, wishing and hoping that I'd only pay. I tell them I'm broke, I haven't a cent, but they don't give a shit, they just want their rent.' This was his prayer day after day, when finally God had something to say. *'I can only do so much from where I sit, so please my son, just buy a ticket.'* One fine Sunday morning Father Mark shared this story in all his glory. Laughs are like blessings thrown all about, here and forever and always throughout.

****

"Hillbillies are the result of the American Indians populating with the Pilgrims."

***

"Laughter is the best medicine."

***

"A wrong decision is better than indecision." Tony Soprano

***

"Remember when I asked for your opinion?—Yeah me either."

***

"Married men live longer than single men, but married men are a lot more willing to die." Johnny Carson

***

"You choose this life; you want to work in the rain try out for the YANKEES." Tony Soprano

***

"Last time I checked—this is not the merry old Land of Oz."

***

"Money may not buy happiness, but I'd rather cry in my CADILLAC than on the bus."

***

"But then, like George Michael in a men's bathroom—I got cocky."

***

"I owe, I owe, it's off to work I go."

***

"I NEED A HUGe amount of money."

***

"Some people are so far behind in the race they think their leading." Junior Soprano

***

"After the Butcher backed into his meat grinder—he got a little behind in his work."

***

"When I was young I was scared of the dark. Now when I see my electric bill—I'm scared of the lights."

***

"James Gandolfini, he didn't really die, he just relocated." RIP6/13/2013

***

"I've been told I'm going to hell for my excessive use of the word FUCK. I have rented a bus if any of your FUCKERS need a ride." (I'm driving)

***

"The oldest computer can be traced back to Adam and Eve. Surprise! Surprise! It was an Apple. But with extremely limited memory, just one byte—then everything crashed."

***

"'If you can quote the rules then you can obey them," Tony Soprano

***

"All my life I kept trying to get up in society. Where everything was higher and legal, but the higher I go the more crooked it became. Where the hell is the end?" Mario Puzo Godfather III

***

"She's crazy, and just when you think you've reached the bottom of her craziness, there's a crazy underground garage."

***

"Grace that blouse hurts like a hangover." Karen Walker

***

"Who picks out your clothes…Stevie Wonder" Don Rickles

***

"Everything will kill you, so choose something fun." Burgess Meredith

***

"Why is Peter Pan always flying—He Neverland's."

***

"I speak my mind because it hurts to bite my tongue."

***

"NASA's Mars Lander found traces of ice and salt on Mars; it's now searching for Tequila" David Letterman

***

"How can money be the root of all evil when shopping is the cure for sadness?"

***

"You're gonna eat lightening and you're gonna crap thunder." Mickey from 'Rocky'

***

"Whenever I have a panic attack I put a brown paper bag to my mouth and drink the vodka inside, it seems to help." Burgess Meredith

***

"If you wear cowboy clothes are you RANCH DRESSING?"

***

"Success is a very good deodorant."

***

"I've been through it all baby, I'm mother courage." Elizabeth Taylor.

***

"Blondes have more fun, only until their roots show."

***

"My pocket-money is in someone else's pants pockets."

***

"There are two sides to every situation, the side you told and the truth."

***

"Try not to mention money today, see how long you can last."

***

"All I'm saying is, you never seen my crying and eating tacos at the same time."

***

"You can take the girl out of the hills, but you can't take the hills out of the girl."

***

"Excuses are like assholes, everybody's got one."

***

"My imaginary friend thinks you have serious mental problems."

***

"I refuse to have a battle of wits with an unarmed person."

***

"Your village called their idiot is missing."

***

"Practice safe sex—go screw-yourself"

***

"Sarcasm just one more service I offer."

***

"You need someone listening to you for it to be an actual conversation."

***

"Fact of life: After Monday and Tuesday even the calendar says W. T. F."

***

"I did not trip. The floor looked sad, so I thought it needed a hug."

***

"When you realize most adults in the world still read this symbol '#' as pound…and you name your woman's movement against sexual harassment #METOO"

***

"Sometimes, when dealing with people, you can't help, but stop and think 'Yup, I'm about to get my first assault charge!'"

***

"If someone treats you like a joke—leave them like it's funny."

***

"What is the German word for Constipation? 'FARFROMPOOPEN'"

***

"Oh, I didn't tell you?—Must have been none of your fucking business then."

***

"Tuesday is just Monday's ugly sister."

***

"This whole thing is pointless, like a Public Defender."

***

♫"And now, the end is near
And so I face the final curtain
My friend, I'll say it clear
I'll state my case, of which I'm certain

I've lived a life that's full
I've traveled each and every highway
But more, much more than this
I did it my way

Regrets, I've had a few
But then again, too few to mention
I did what I had to do
And saw it through without exemption

I planned each charted course
Each careful step along the byway
And more, much more than this
I did it my way."♪

Frank Sinatra

Chapter 3. Things my mother told me

Mom made it look easy, she was witty and smart. She married a musician and followed her heart. Some days we struggled, most days were fine, but who doesn't face adversity from time to time. Her generation survived, the Second World War, sadly her family overseas are no more. Mom believed in the church, and the goodness in everything, maybe that's why she never stopped learning. Our home was filled with good times and cheer, hoping and praying throughout the year. Her love and care will never us part as I look back on these things Ma shared from her heart. Mom left us reasons, and made life fun, she made us proud, of where we came from.

Mom's last words were...

"Everyone better go to Church"

□ □ □ □

"If you have to lose your head, at least hold your tongue."

□ □ □

"You'll know who really loves you if they let you eat first, if they ask you if you ate and if they gave you to eat" mom

□ □ □

"My mother raised me to be admired."

☐ ☐ ☐

"Fish and houseguest go bad after 3 days."

☐ ☐ ☐

"I sent my daughter to Europe and she came back without a husband, I'm dying" mom

☐ ☐ ☐

"One thing you still get for a penny—your thoughts."

☐ ☐ ☐

"New York is a city without coincidence."

☐ ☐ ☐

"Buying what you don't need leads to needing what you can't buy."

☐ ☐ ☐

"We're better off if we act our wage."

☐ ☐ ☐

"There is a love that never ends…Moms"

☐ ☐ ☐

"Wise people don't find life worthwhile, they make it worthwhile."

☐ ☐ ☐

"Don't just try. Anyone can try. DO IT"

◻ ◻ ◻

"Listen to MOM, she's been there and she's done that."

◻ ◻ ◻

"The great and powerful MOM has spoken."

◻ ◻ ◻

"Two empty heads are better than one."

◻ ◻ ◻

"Mothers just know—children have no clue."

◻ ◻ ◻

"A mothers spit can clean...ANYTHING."

◻ ◻ ◻

"If mom could teach me half of what she knows, I would be a happy woman."

◻ ◻ ◻

"I've been described as the brains of my father and the wit of my mother."

◻ ◻ ◻

"You can fool some of the people some of the time, but you can't fool MOM" The Little Rascals

◻ ◻ ◻

"A man can have as many women as he wants, but he will only have one mother."

❑ ❑ ❑

"You can't talk and listen at the same time."

❑ ❑ ❑

"Beauty is in the mirror."

❑ ❑ ❑

"God gave us parents to carry out his message."

❑ ❑ ❑

"So tell me again, how are we related?"

❑ ❑ ❑

"Would you rather look dumb and ask for help or remain dumb?"

❑ ❑ ❑

"Only a family can make a house a home."

❑ ❑ ❑

"The Secret of a good woman is to bring out the best in a man."

❑ ❑ ❑

"Once you cross that line, you can never go back."

❑ ❑ ❑

"Doing the right thing is not always the popular thing."

❑ ❑ ❑

"A stitch in time saves nine."

□ □ □

"New York City is my state of mind."

□ □ □

"Love is love, but Business is BUSINESS."

□ □ □

"Flowers are for weddings and funerals, every other occasion jewelry works best."

□ □ □

"Surround yourself with the dreamers and the doers, the believers and the thinkers, but most of all; surround yourself with those who see greatness within you, even when you don't see it in yourself."

□ □ □

My wish for you:

"When you are lonely I wish you love. When you are down, I wish you joy, when you are troubled, I wish you peace. When things look empty, I wish you hope. May you be surrounded by Happiness, Peace and Joy."

□ □ □

"Be with someone who is not only proud to have you, but will take every risk just to keep you."

□ □ □

"Food is the only beautiful thing that truly nourishes."

□ □ □

"Talk is cheap, don't buy into it."

□ □ □

"When attending a party, always eat home first."

□ □ □

"Mom maybe going blind, but she see's people for who they are."

□ □ □

"Sooner or later—we all quote our mothers."

□ □ □

♫"Once upon a time there was a tavern
Where we used to raise a glass or two
Remember how we laughed away the hours
And think of all the great things we would do

Those were the days my friend
We thought they'd never end
We'd sing and dance forever and a day
We'd live the life we choose
We'd fight and never lose
For we were young and sure to have our way"♪

Chapter 4. Touching Quotes and antidotes

When I started URS in 1992, I spoke with a man who was tried and true. An avid traveler so kind and sincere, outspoken of his journeys both far and near. He proceeded to explain just what it means, for him to have all these Travel Magazines. He was quite proud to share how they took him to places, from the people, the regions and even their faces. After some time he confided in me, that he was dying of cancer, *oh no not thee.* Not knowing what to say, he quickly came to my aide, 'here is my visa, please mark me paid.'

I did as he asked and processed his request, not knowing how much time this poor fella had left. He spent his money on what brought him joy and laughter. I don't remember his name, but this remained with me hereafter…

"Everyone must see San Diego before they die."

****

"A girl should be two things CLASSY & FABULOUS" Coco Chanel

***

"A man, who doesn't spend time with his family, can never be a real man." John Gotti

***

"Sometimes the best way to throw a punch is to take a step back." Morgan Freeman

***

"Jealousy is a good indication that you are doing things the right way. People never get jealous of losers."

***

"Words honor a man, but an action is what crowns him." James Bond

***

"Man gives the award—God gives the reward."

***

"Don't smoke in bed the ashes that fall maybe your own."

***

"My home is in America, but my heart belongs to Paris."

***

"And though she be but little, she is Fierce" Shakespeare

***

"You can't beat a person who never gives up."

***

"Never be controlled by three things: your past, money or people."

***

"I'm only responsible for what I say, not for what you understand." John Wayne

***

"I don't know how I am going to win; I just know I am not going to lose."

***

"How do we change the world—one random act of kindness at a time," Morgan Freeman

***

"Anyone can make war, but only the most courageous can make peace."

***

"Success is the ability to go from failure to failure without losing your enthusiasm." Winston Churchill

***

"We cannot all do great things, but we can do small things with great love." Mother Theresa

***

"Luxury must be comfortable; otherwise it's not a luxury."
Coco Chanel

***

"Trust the wait. Embrace the uncertainty. Enjoy the beauty of becoming. When nothing is certain, anything is possible."

***

"If you begin, YOU WIN."

***

"Pour yourself a drink, put on some lipstick, and pull yourself together." Elizabeth Taylor

***

"The world tells us to seek success, power and money; God tells us to seek humanity, service and love." Pope Francis

***

"Be careful with your words, once they are said, they can only be forgiven, not forgotten."

***

"Normality is a paved road: it's comfortable to walk, but no flowers grow." Vincent van Gogh

***

"If you want to be original, be prepared to be copied." Coco Chanel

***

"You're not supposed to understand everything." Rod Steiger

***

"Surround yourself with people that reflect who you want to be and how you want to feel, energies are contagious." Rachel Wolchin

***

"The fruit of silence is prayer. The fruit of prayer is faith. The fruit of faith is love. The fruit of love is service. The fruit of service is peace." Canonized 9/4/2016 Blessed Teresa of Calcutta

***

"Time is very slow for those who wait. Very fast for those who are scared. Very long for those who lament. Very short for those who celebrate, but for those who love, time is eternal." William Shakespeare

***

"If you want to SOAR in life you must first learn to F.L.Y. (first love yourself)."

***

"Never think that you're not good enough. A man should never think that. My belief is that in life, people will take you at your own reckoning." Isaac Asimov

***

"Success is most often achieved by those who don't know that failure is inevitable." Coco Chanel

***

"Trust your instincts. Your mistakes might as well be your own instead of someone else's." Billy Wilder

***

"I don't count my sit-ups. I only start counting when it starts hurting. When I feel pain, that's when I start counting, because that's when it really counts." Muhammad Ali

***

"Trust your GUT." Barbara Walters

***

"Why waste your time looking up your family tree, just go into politics and your opponent will do it for you." Mark Twain

***

"If you run into a wall, don't turn around and give up. Figure out how to climb it, go through it, or work around it." Michael Jordan best basketball player ever

***

"Mistakes are the portals of discovery." James Joyce

***

"My favorite words are possibilities, opportunities and curiosity. I think if you are curious, you create opportunities, and then if you open the doors, you create possibilities." Mario Testino

***

"My life cost Jesus his…John 15:13"

***

"Here's to strong women—may we know them, May we be them and May we raise them." The Duchess

***

"Yesterday I was clever, so I wanted to change the world. Today I am wise, so I am changing myself." Rumi

***

"It never gets easier, you just get BETTER."

***

"No one can change TRUTH."

***

"Work like a CAPTAIN, play like a PIRATE."

***

"Swag is just …**Stuff We All Get**."

***

"I'll treat you so good, you'll never want to let me go." Julia Roberts Pretty Woman

***

"If you can't pronounce it, you can't afford it!"

***

"Shakespeare was right, ENGLISH is hard."

***

"I'd rather be scared by my efforts, than never learn to ride."

***

"It isn't where you came from that counts, it's where you're going that matters" Ella Fitzgerald

***

"My idea of Food, Clothing and Shelter is moms cooking, Bloomingdales and the Hotel Ritz in Paris."

***

"The girl next door ran away with the boy from the wrong side of the tracks and they lived happily-ever-after."

***

"Fool me once, shame on you; fool me twice, shame on me."

***

"If time is on my side, the clocked stopped."

***

"Walt Disney, it all started with a dream."

***

"If you put a price tag on moms it would read PRICELESS."

***

"You're like a light bulb just waiting to be screwed."

***

"Wherever you stand, be the soul of that place." Rumi

***

"You meet approximately 12 serial killers in your lifetime without knowing it."

***

"Whosoever is delighted in solitude is either a wild beast or a God" Aristotle

***

"When looking for beauty use a mirror instead of a telescope."

***

"Instead of looking at the sawdust on the floor—look at the flowers on the table," Gwen Darnall

***

"Every woman must have a purse of her own." Susan B. Anthony

***

"Kill them with success and bury them with a smile." Sandeep Kumar

***

"People will stare. Make it worth their while."

***

"I'm not paid enough to kiss your ass."

***

"As long as you have a book, you are never alone." LC

***

"Don't get mad get everything" Ivana Trump.

***

"Let go of the thoughts that don't make you strong."

***

"Live life as if everything is rigged in your favor."

***

"Every time I look at a keyboard I see 'U' and 'I' are always together."

***

"We do not remember days, we remember moments."

***

"When you give a lot of importance to someone in your life you lose importance in your life."

***

"Never cry for that person who never knew the value of your tears…"

***

"Do not love a friend who hurts you…and do not hurt a friend who loves you. Sacrifice everything for a friend, but do not ever sacrifice a friend for anything."

***

"Life is like photography, we develop from the negatives."

***

"Love your parents we are so busy growing up; we often forget
they are growing old."

***

♫"I'm trying so hard to forget you.
And leave the life we had behind.
And there are times I feel the day has come,
I've chased you from my mind.

But I'm afraid there's always something,
That sets me back and makes me see.
You're more than just a memory in the past,
You're still a part of me.

So how do I stop loving you?
Forget things that we used to do?
Forget all the dreams that we shared?
And how my life was knowing you cared?
Why do I end up where I start, each time I try?

Just tell me how I can forget,
So I can say goodbye."♪

Barry Manilow

Chapter 5.The Truth Comes out when you drink

I don't trust anyone who exclaims they don't drink, a statement that defines, more than you think. Business meetings will gather from far and near, to conduct their business over an icy cold beer. Families will gather at a bar or around the table to deal with anything, ready willingly and able. Wars are resolved and ties will bind, over some sort of spirit, a cocktail or wine. Take comfort in knowing there's nothing to fear when Stoli's, Johnnie Walker, or Jack Daniels are near. Whether you meet at a bar, or a fine restaurant, drinks with friends, and become fine confidents.

****

"No one ever got drunk on the word wine alone, you have to experience it." Father Mark Dinardo

***

"Never trust a man who doesn't drink." Humphrey Bogart

***

"I'd rather be someone's shot of whiskey than everyone's cup of tea."

***

"3 things to know in life, never beg anyone, never trust no one, never expect anything from anybody."

***

"If you drink don't drive—don't even putt." Dean Martin

***

"The SKY's the limit—Sky Vodka that is."

***

"Are you okay? I never know until I sober up." Charlie Harper

***

"You're not drunk if you can lie on the floor without holding on" Dean Martin

***

"Everybody's a gangster, until a gangster walks in the room." John Gotti

***

"Beer is proof God loves us and wants us to be happy." Benjamin Franklin

***

"Friends are like flowers give them a drink and watch them bloom."

***

"Have a drink—it will make me look younger."

***

"I'm an 'old fashioned' and you're the cherry."

***

"It's not called slurring your words—it's called talking in cursive." Dean Martin

***

"Alcohol is poison, then why do you drink it—because there are things inside me that I need to kill." Charlie Harper

***

"Titanic: when she said 'Jack I'll never let you go, I think she meant Jack Daniels,"

***

"I drink, therefore I am drunk."

***

"These days I think even my guardian angel drinks."

***

"I wish I could trade my heart for another liver, that way I can drink more and care-less." Tina Fey

***

"I feel sorry for people who don't drink—they wake up in the morning and that's the best they're going to feel all day." Dean Martin

***

"I got jumped last night by some Russian gangster Smirnoff, a ship captain named Morgan and redneck called Jack Daniels. Bastards nailed me."

***

"You say Potato, I say Vodka." Karen Walker

***

"Drinking rum before 10:00AM makes you a PIRATE not an ALCOHOLIC,"

***

"You can't drink all day if you don't start in the morning."

***

"Sippity doo dah—Sippity yay!"

***

"Friends don't let friends go thirsty."

***

"Whiskey, because who the hell needs feelings."

***

"Of all the gin joints in all the towns, in all the world, she walks into mine." Bogart

***

"Don't say I'm difficult to shop for, you know where the liquor store is."

***

"Whenever the brain and the heart fight it's always the liver that suffers."

***

"I don't drink any more than the man next to me and the man next to me is Dean Martin."

***

"If you don't drink, how will your friends know you love them at 2AM?"

***

"I drink to make other people more interesting." Ernest Hemingway

***

"Be Good or Be Gone." McSorley's Old Ale House

***

"I don't drink alcohol, I drink distilled spirits. Therefore I'm not an alcoholic I'm spiritual." Dean Martin

***

"You bring the alcohol; I'll bring the bad decisions."

***

"According to chemistry alcohol is a solution."

***

"I have mixed drinks about feelings."

***

"Drink happy thoughts."

***

"Ashes to ashes, dust to dust. When life's a bitch Vodka's a must."

***

"'What's your nationality?' 'I'm a drunkard…'" Casablanca

***

"Why limit happy to an hour?"

***

"Never take advice from me, you'll end up drunk."

***

"I got so drunk last night, I walked across the dance floor to get another drink and won the dance contest."

***

"Hakuna Ma'Vodka"

***

"I don't remember much from last night, but the fact that I needed sunglasses to open the fridge this morning tells me it was awesome."

***

"Put your hair up in a bun, drink some Gin and regret nothing."

***

"When people say they don't need alcohol to have fun, all I hear is designated driver."

***

"I drank so much Vodka last night I woke up with a Russian Accent."

***

"Tonight, I'll be having my favorite drink
It's called—A LOT."

***

"Every empty bottle is filled with stories."

***

"Tonight I'm drinking until I'm someone else's problem."

***

"There is only one thing better than a glass of champagne
A BOTTLE."

***

"Vodka is kind of a hobby." Betty White

***

"I do not get drunk, I get AWESOME."

***

"In wine there is wisdom, in beer there is freedom, in water there is bacteria."

***

"You're not really drinking alone if your dog is home."

***

"I'd love to take you out for coffee this week."
"You spelled WINE wrong."

***

"I think I said I'd have 2 glasses of wine and be home by 8.
I always get those two mixed-up."

***

"You went from being my drug to the reason I need them."

***

"When people ask me what I did over the weekend. I always
squint and reply…why what did you hear?"

***

"The answer may not lie at the bottom of a beer bottle, but you
should always check."

***

"We have an open door policy. Show up with wine, and we'll
open the door."

***

"Education is important but beer is imported."

***

"Another wine bottle emptied with no GENIE at the bottom.
The search continues…"

***

"Wine is like duct tape, it fixes everything."

***

"Working nine to wine,"

***

"You were my cup of tea, but I drink wine now."

***

"Alcohol! Because no great story ever began with—a salad,"

***

"To me 'drink responsibly' means don't spill it."

***

"I will drink BEER here or I will drink BEER there, I will
drink my BEER everywhere." Cat in the Hat

***

"There is something so wonderful about drinking in the
afternoon." Anthony Bourdain RIP suicide 6/8/18

***

"The next time you order KALE, try with a silent 'K' it taste
much better."

***

"Barley makes beer, apples make apple cider, potatoes make
vodka, sugarcane makes Rum and grapes make wine. You
can't get smashed without Farmers, you're welcome." Rebecca
and Jimmy Modock

***

"Look at the size of your liver compared to your heart. You are designed to drink more and care less."

***

"Whiskey is spelled with an 'E'. Just like Freedom, Liberty, and America."

***

"Good judgment comes from experience, and experience— well that comes from poor judgment."

***

"Today's Soup: Whiskey with Ice Croutons."

***

"Whiskey—you old devil friend."

***

"Bourbon—my only company in solitude."

***

"Happy Birthday!" (I was going to drink anyway)

***

"Rule #1 Fuck what they think."

***

"Twenty-four hours in a day, twenty-four beers in a case, you do the math."

***

"Stop trying to make everyone happy—you're not TEQUILA."

***

"I only drink wine on days that end in 'Y.' "

***

"Life is not a fairytale, if you lose your shoes at midnight.
You're fucking drunk."

***

"Could you keep it down, I'm trying to drink."

***

"The problem with the world is everyone is a few drinks
behind," Liz Taylor

***

"Alcohol is the anesthesia by which we endure the operation of
life." George Bernard Shaw

***

"Shut up liver, your fine,"

***

"When life hands you lemons, make Whiskey Sours."
W.C Fields.

***

"You get sloppy drunk, I stay whiskey neat."

***

"Laughter maybe the best medicine, but Jack Daniels makes a
pretty good Band-Aid."

***

"Jack doesn't ask silly questions, Jack understands."

***

"MR. Jack Daniels passed away due to an injury he sustained when kicking his safe early one morning at work. Moral to the story—never go into work early."

***

"In wine there is wisdom, in beer there is strength, but in whiskey lies the water of life."

***

"Vodka for the ladies and whiskey for the grown-men,"

***

"Whiskey: the nighttime sniffling, sneezing, how the hell did I end up on the bathroom floor medicine."

***

"Alcohol may be man's worst enemy, but the bible says love your enemy." Frank Sinatra

***

"I didn't text you…VODKA did!"

***

"Here's to cheating, stealing, fighting and drinking; if you cheat, cheat death. If you steal, may you steal a woman's heart; if you fight, may you fight for a brother, and if you must drink, drink with me."

***

"Roses are red, violets are blue,
whiskey cost less than dinner for two."

***

"Girls are made of sugar & spice but I'm a bit more
complicated, I'm made of whisky and ice."

***

"A little bit of honey and a whole lot of Jack."

***

"Whiskey and Ice and everything nice,"

***

"A shot of whiskey in the old west: .45 cartridge for a six-gun
cost 12cents, so did a glass of whiskey. If a cowhand was low
on cash he would often give the bartender a cartridge in
exchange for a drink. This became known as a 'SHOT' of
whiskey."

***

"This Vodka taste like—I'm not going to work tomorrow."

***

"How's that beer tasting?—like the first of many."

***

"All dressed up in a pretty black label, sweet salvation on a
dining room table, waiting on me, where the numb meets the
lonely, the shot is gone before it melts the ice." Miranda
Lambert

***

"To the times you'll never remember, with the people you'll never forget."

***

"Too much of anything is bad, but too much of a good whiskey is barely enough." Mark Twain

***

"Four drinks and I'm using FUCK like a comma."

***

"I'm in a good place right now, not emotionally, I'm just at the liquor store."

***

"E-Harmony matched me up with Jack Daniels."

***

"You know those little butterflies you get when you're in love; well Jack Daniels shuts them up quite well."

***

"Friday just called she'll be here tomorrow and she's bringing the VODKA."

***

"When I was little I had a Jack-in-the-box, now I prefer my Jack- in-a-bottle."

***

"This house runs best on LOVE, LAUGHTER
& Jack Daniels."

***

"I'm for anything that gets you through the night, be it prayer,
tranquilizers, or a bottle of Jack Daniels." Frank Sinatra

***

"This whiskey taste like I'm about to tell you how I really
feel."

***

"I'm lost somewhere between Jack Daniels and Jesus."

***

"Beware of woman with their eyes somewhere else."
Louie Lacey

***

"Roses, Chanel and Champagne, can get you through most
anything."

***

"The doctor said I need to drink more whiskey, I'm now
calling myself the doctor."

***

"Whiskey probably won't fix your problems,
but hell it's worth a SHOT."

***

"Open your BEERs, close your APPs." Stella Artois

***

"Whiskey makes me Frisky."

***

"Every day we make it, we'll make it the best we can"
Jack Daniels

***

"Whiskey is what beer wants to be when it grows up."

***

"Now I lay me down to sleep, a bottle at my feet, if I die before
I wake, tell my friends I drank it straight."

***

"Take the time to ENJOY and ENJOY the time you take."
Stella Artois

***

"I only drink champagne on two occasions, when I am in
LOVE and when I am not." Coco Chanel

***

"Lower your distractions raise your challis." Stella Artois

***

"I don't drink to get drunk. I drink to get my inner demons
drunk, so they'll pass out and give me some peace."

***

"If troubles were money, I'd be filthy rich."

***

"A little wine makes business better."

***

"Sip, sip…Hurray."

***

"Never walk a mile in my shoes. You'll just end up DRUNK, LOST and looking for your shoes."

***

"When infatuation wears real, love begins"

***

"Why is a man who invests your money called a BROKER?"

***

"What do people in China call their good plates?"

***

"When dad died the days grew-long, we grew-up, then a blessing was sent we called her Tiffany."

***

"There are just some girls you can't drink pretty."

***

"Now that I'm old enough to drink, the one person I wanted to drink with is gone…my dad."

***

"Raise a glass: To Health and Friendship to life and love, not to forget blessing from above."

***

"Scotch Tape- stuck on the drink."

***

"Don't save the best for last."

***

"I want to meet Jack Daniels and thank him for giving me the courage to do almost anything."

***

"Those who have a few QUICK ONES are sure to have a few close ones."

***

"Philosophy is the last refuge of thinkers."

***

"Most likely to couple—A couple of drinks, a couple of kids, a couple of bills and a couple of aspirin."

***

"Rain, Sleet and Snow, a reminder that we shall never be thirsty,"

***

"I don't drink, I don't swear and I don't smoke…God damn it, I left my cigarettes at the bar." Louis Lacey

***

"The many phases of my day: Bloody Mary's, to wake me up, Cosmopolitans over lunch then Shots and Brandy, till last call."

***

"Candy is dandy but liquor is quicker." Willy Wonka

***

"I'll have a Tequila-Sunrise-Sunset."

***

"Sometimes you gotta be saved from yourself."

***

"Not for more years, Four MORE BEERS."

***

"Me and the outdoors don't mix."

***

"The Boys of summer, Johnnie Walker, Jim Beam, Jack Daniels,"

***

"You are giving me a Harvey Wall-banger of a headache."

***

"Some nights I drink tea, some nights long island iced tea."

***

"If the world was an ocean and I was a duck, I would swim to the bottom, than I'd swim my way up, but the world is not an ocean and I am not a duck—so let's drink this shot and get all fucked-up."

***

"One should always have Champagne in their refrigerator for life's little celebrations."

***

"One martini, two martini, three martini—FLOOR."

***

"The boys in blue… BOMBAY SAPHIRE & SKY VODKA."

***

"A secret is something you tell one person at a time."

***

"Stop the world—I want to get off."

***

"People who stand in your way, have no direction."

***

"Red is short for READY."

***

"Don't worry I'm not dangerous, I didn't drink enough yet."

***

"Let me ask you this—are you nuts?"

***

"I put all my eggs in one basket and made an omelet."

***

"When you get even with a person,
you come down to their level."

***

"Crazy is just another word for OPINIATED."

***

"It ain't cheating unless you get caught."

***

"To be with another woman is FRENCH—to be with another
woman and get caught is AMERICAN."

***

"College is a career; it's your JOB to do well."

***

"Would you rather be pissed-on or doing the pissing?"

***

"Stop the thinking—let's start drinking!"

***

"I want a drunk of my own."

***

"I used to think drinking was bad for me, so I gave up
thinking."

***

"You'll never work a day in your life, if you love what you do."

***

"Golfer: a drunken liar, in ugly pants, who plays with his balls in public."

***

"Those who think they know it all, are on the road to HELL."

***

"When it comes to PRO's and CON's remember you're in the middle"

***

"Did the Wizard ever get back to you about that brain thing?"

***

"Mothers of little boys work from Son up till Son down,"

***

"How can you go from NYC to London to Paris then out to Vegas and never leave your home? The telephone"

***

"Americans pride themselves on the pursuit of happiness."

***

"Playing the lottery give you the right to dream and the chance to win, all for just $1.00."

***

"I'm hopelessly flawed."

***

"What is the difference between beer nuts and deer nuts—deer nuts are under a BUCK,"

***

"Tipping is a reflection of your character."

***

"Johnny Carson is and will always be the King of Late-night."

***

"I think I just got the goodbye look."

***

"A lie is not a lie when feelings are spared."

***

"You can't be everything to everyone."

***

"The Luck is gone, the brain is shot, the Liquor we still got!"

***

"One is too few and one hundred is not enough."
The Lost Weekend

***

"Engine room, where the hell's my drink,"

***

"Haven't you had enough—I want more than enough,"

***

"I finally quit drinking for GOOD, now I drink for EVIL."

***

"You're such a disaster—
the Red Cross won't even give you coffee."

***

"You had to come in all high and mighty, Acting all mighty
while I was high."

***

"Drink with me I make life more fun."

***

"A man's true character comes out when he's drunk."

***

"Friends are like condoms they protect you when thing get
hard,"

***

"Alcohol will not solve your problems.
Then again neither will MILK."

***

"Age gets better with wine."

Chapter 6. Music Notes and Quotes

My grandfather was a bass player it was all that he knew, my father was a bass player, it got him through. My brother's a bass player most of the time, and my nephew is a bass player on his downtime. My world was a soundtrack made of many different tunes; many different genera's that filled every room. I believe my father's God given talent was to be a musician, because he was not just good at it; it became his ambition. With great discipline, he mastered Brahms and Mozart, but it was the jazz of the day that pulled at his heart. From the Jazz in the 60's right downtown, Cleveland was a place where so much music was found. The Theatrical was Jazz at its best, while Severance Hall housed the elitist. Dad filled our home with music you see, songs and melodies while we trimmed the tree. Birthdays, dinners, parties and such, music just adds that perfect touch. Even though Dad is gone, his melodies still linger on. Sometimes it's nice to just pour a drink, to listen to dad—to ponder to think.

♫♪♫♪♫♪

♫♪♫

"When I first heard Frank Sinatra sing he flew me to the moon
and I've been amongst the stars ever since."

♫♪♫

"Music touches us emotionally—when words alone can't."
Johnny Depp

♫♪♫

"Music is the only universal language."

♫♪♫

♫"You'll never find peace of mind until you listen to your
heart."♪ George Michael

♫♪♫

"To be is to do—Socrartes.
To do is to be—Jean-Paul Sartre.
Do be do be do—Sinatra."

♫♪♫

"Love, peace and music," Crystal Horvath

♫♪♫

"I couldn't carry a tune if it had a handle."

♫♪♫

"I've started a band called 999 mega bites—
we haven't gotten a gig yet."

♫♪♫

"Fact: one of the only activities that activate, stimulates and uses the entire brain is MUSIC."

♫♪♫

"What did one guitar say to the other guitar—I always feel like I'm being played."

♫♪♫

"Life is like a piano; the white keys represent happiness and the black shows sadness, but as you go through life's journey, remember that the black keys also make music."

♫♪♫

"Don't cry for me, for I will go where Music is born" J. S. Bach

♫♪♫

"One good thing about MUSIC, when it hits you— you feel no pain."

♫♪♫

"Geology class: name the 3 types of rock, Classic, Punk and Hard."

♫♪♫

"Opera is when a Tenor and Soprano want to make love, but are prevented from doing so by a Baritone."

♫♪♫

"If you have to ask what Jazz is—you'll never know."

♫♪♫

"I still believe that Music is one of the greatest gifts
God gave to man." George Michael
(died on Christmas day 2016, his song 'Last Christmas'
became a fulfilling prophecy.)

♬♪♬

"I keep hearing music from the printer—I think the paper is
jamming."

♬♪♬

"George [Michael], I want your sex, so be my father figure and
I will have faith if we have to live hand-to-mouth."
Madonna Ciccone

♬♪♬

"There is no top. There are always further heights to reach."
Jascha Heifetz (violinist)

***

"I should be sorry, if I only entertain them. I wish to make
them better." Georg Frideric Handel

***

"If you possess something, but you can't give it away, then you
don't possess it…it possesses you." Frank Sinatra

***

"The big lesson in life baby, in never be scared of anyone or
anything." Sinatra

***

♫"Smile though your heart is aching, smile even though it's breaking…"♪ Charlie Chaplin

♫♪♫

"Wild is the music of autumnal winds amongst the faded woods." William Wordsworth

♫♪♫

♫"If I should lose you, the stars would fall from the sky…"♪

♫♪♫

"Close your eyes and let the music set you free." Phantom of the Opera

♫♪♫

"I'm gonna live till I die…" Sinatra

***

"No regrets, although our love affair has gone astray," Ella Fitzgerald

♫♪♫

"NO music—no life." Pauly D

♫♪♫

"When you are happy, you enjoy the music. But when you are sad, you understand the lyrics."

♫♪♫

♫"The very thought of you makes my heart sing…"♪Sting

***

"Music produces a kind of pleasure that human nature cannot do without."

♫♪♫

"If I can make it there, I can make it anywhere it's up to you New York, New York…" Sinatra

♫♪♫

"If you let a person talk long enough you'll hear their true intentions. Listen twice, speak once." Tupac RIP 1996

♫♪♫

"Tonight could be the best nigh of your life" the house of blues

♫♪♫

"In the wee small hours of the morning—that's the time I miss her most of all" Frank Sinatra

♫♪♫

"You can't touch music, but music can touch you."

♫♪♫

"For all we know, we may never meet again."

♫♪♫

"Falling in love with love is falling for make-believe." Sammy Davis Jr.

♫♪♫

"All of us contain music and truth, but most of us can't get it out" Mark Twain

♫♪♫

"You'll never find another love like mine…" Lou Rawls

♫♪♫

"Broadway—land of a thousand scores,"

♫♪♫

"Death is not the greatest loss in life. The greatest loss is what dies inside while still alive. Never Surrender" Tupac RIP 1996

♫♪♫

"Dream on, dream until your dreams become true." Aerosmith

♫♪♫

"There are no shortcuts to any place worth going," Beverly Sills

♫♪♫

"if Music be the food of love—play on."

♫♪♫

"All it takes is one song to bring back a thousand memories."

♫♪♫

"If you count watching Elmer Fudd singing 'Kill the Wabbit' then yes I've been to the Opera."

♫♪♫

"Wise men say only fools rush in, but I can't help falling in love with you," Elvis

♫♪♫

"KEEP CALM and fight for music education,"

♫♪♫

"When I teach others, I teach myself" Itzhak Perlman

♫♪♫

"Once you replace negative thoughts with positive ones, you'll start having positive results" Willie Nelson

♫♪♫

"Nothing is as important as passion, no matter what you do with your life, be passionate." Jon Bon Jovi

♫♪♫

"Music is a Moral Law; it gives Soul to the universe" Plato

♫♪♫

"Let me try again, think of all we had before, let me try once more." Frank Sinatra

♫♪♫

"You never know how strong you are, until being strong is your only choice." Bob Marley

♫♪♫

"You are what you listen to."

♫♪♫

"Love, love, love that is the soul of genius," Mozart

♫♪♫

"Bach gave us Gods word. Mozart gave us God's laugher, Beethoven gave us Gods fire. God gave us music that we might pray without words."

♬♪♫

"When I am completely myself, entirely alone—or during the night when I cannot sleep, it is on such occasions that my ideas flow best and most abundantly." Mozart

♬♪♫

"Dear Music, I will never be able to thank you enough for always being there for me."

♬♪♫

"I want to turn off the lights and think of you…" Luis Miguel

♬♪♫

"We're all alone, no chaperon, can't get our number, the world is a slumber—let's misbehave." Cole Porter

♬♪♫

"You're a melody from a symphony by Strauss"

♬♪♫

"When you hit a wrong note, it's the next note that makes it good or bad." Miles Davis

♬♪♫

"People want to hear songs with the words they are afraid to say."

♬♪♫

"Long shower, Loud Music, Deep thoughts."

♬♪♫

"Behind every favorite song, there is an untold story."

♫♪♫

"When words fail, music speaks." Shakespeare

♫♪♫

"Music: the moments, the memories, the pain, the happiness."

♫♪♫

"I play the notes as they are written, but it is GOD who makes the music." J.S. Bach

♫♪♫

"Music is a piece of art that goes in the ear and straight to the heart."

♫♪♫

"The music is not in the notes, but in the silence in-between." Mozart

♫♪♫

"If you are not doing what you love, you are wasting your time." Billy Joel

♫♪♫

"Master your instrument, master your music, then forget all of that and just play." Charlie Parker

♫♪♫

"Those who wish to sing, find their song."

♫♪♫

"To sing is to pray twice." St. Augustine

♫♪♫

"I can't explain, but I will find a song that can."

♫♪♫

"Yesterday I heard the rain whispering your name, asking where you'd gone." Tony Bennett

♫♪♫

"Here's to the best—it's yet to come." Frank Sinatra

♫♪♫

"Night and Day you are the one." Cole Porter

♫♪♫

"The summer wind came blowing in from across the sea; it lingered there touched your hair and walked with me." Johnny Mercer

♫♪♫

"My life, my love, my valentine..." Martina McBride

♫♪♫

"If it takes forever, I will wait for you." Michele Legrand

♫♪♫

"The human race is a symphony, God is the conductor."

♫♪♫

"You put a move on my heart." Tamia

♫♪♫

"Make it one for my baby and one more for the road."

♫♪♫

"Every happy plot ends with a marriage knot."

♫♪♫

"The Lord bless you and keep you." John Rudder

♫♪♫

"I guess I loved you—but I lied."

♫♪♫

"Sometimes it feels like you and me against the world." Helen Ready.

♫♪♫

"When words fail Music Speaks,"

♫♪♫

"Rap music used to be about a message, now it's all about marketing."

♫♪♫

"When autumn leaves start to fall—I miss you most of all." Joseph Kosma

♫♪♫

"The Secret to driving: good tunes on the radio and miss every car." Dad

♫♪♫

"Music is the soundtrack of your life,"

♫♪♫

"I love the fine way he plays a STEINWAY."

♫♪♫

"When you deprive a child of Music you rob them of discovering their hidden talents."

♫♪♫

"It's either STEINWAY or the highway."

♫♪♫

"Music is the shorthand of emotion. Leo Tolstoy"

♫♪♫

"Even as deaf as Beethoven was, he still heard the music resonate."

♫♪♫

"Sooner or later, you're gonna have to face the music."

♫♪♫

"Where would a Violin be without strings attached?"

♫♪♫

"Music feeds the soul as well as the mind."

♫♪♫

"Please leave the singing to the professionals."

♫♪♫

"Support the arts, sleep with a musician."

♫♪♫

"Ain't no sunshine—when she's gone."

♫♪♫

"Some people are so poor, all they have is money." Bob
Marley

♫♪♫

"Classical music is an acquired taste."

♫♪♫

"Music is like sex, some people like it deep and emotional.
Some people like it soft it floats, and some people like it hard
and banging."

♫♪♫

"When the pain penetrates—the music resonates."

♫♪♫

"I like New York in June, April in Paris and Autumn Leaves."

♫♪♫

"You don't know what love is—until you learn the meaning of
the blues."

♫♪♫

"Listen; there is a song for every situation."

♫♪♫

"Sinatra had a comeback in every decade."

♫♪♫

"Dad always called us kids his 'treble—makers'."

♫♪♫

"Musicians never die they just De-compose."

♫♪♫

"Music is a drug that doesn't require a prescription."

♫♪♫

"With music I can be whatever and I can be where ever I want."

♫♪♫

"Music soothes the savage beast."

***

"To be a musician, you must have the spirit of a gypsy and the discipline of a soldier." Beethoven

♫♪♫

"Music is life. That's why our hearts have beats."

♫♪♫

"To play a wrong note is insignificant; to play without passion is inexcusable."

♫♪♫

"Through the years the sweetest days I found with you" Kenny Rogers

***

"I faced it all and I stood tall and did it my way." Frank Sinatra

***

♫"Go on your way with the cloudless blue sky above
May all your days be a wonderful song of love
Open your arms and sing of all the hidden hopes you'll ever
treasure
And live out your life in peace

Where shall I look for the love to replace you
Someone to light up my life
Someone with strange little ways
Eyes like a blue autumn haze
Someone with your laughing style
And a smile that I know will keep haunting me endlessly

Sometimes in stars or the swift flight of seabirds
I catch a moment of you
That's why I walk all alone
Searching for something unknown
Searching for something or someone to light up my life."♪

Sinatra

Chapter 7. Age, Life and Longevity

*I love **my age.**
Old enough to
know better. Young
enough not to care.
Experienced enough
to **do it right.***

When you reach a certain age, you have certain expectations, some require vision, but most a solid foundation. Life is a present; simple, humble or grand, just keep in mind it's all in your hand. Longevity is not promised, nor can you buy, but with age comes wisdom, don't let life pass you by. Age is a miracle, life is a gift, but longevity my friends is what you make out of it.

****

"Age is just a number if you believe it, you'll feel it."

***

"Worry less, smile more."

***

"May your Angel guard your door and allow only joy and love to come into your house."

***

"At my age, seen it all, done it all, and heard it all—I just can't remember it all."

***

"If you can't explain it to a six year old, you don't understand it yourself." Albert Einstein

***

"Do something today that your future self will thank you for."

***

"Wise men talk because they have something to say; fools, because they have to say something." Plato

***

"If ignorance is bliss why aren't there more happy people?"

***

"You are better when you don't think so deeply" Ernest Hemingway, 'A farewell To Arms'

***

"Take time to make your soul happy."

***

"Don't make more money than a man, if you do—lie to him." Pamela Anderson Lee

***

"We are here to laugh at the odds and live our lives so well that death will tremble to take us." Charles Bukowski

***

"Find what you love to do, then figure out how to get paid for it."

***

"Listen to GOD and don't rewrite his job description."

***

"A mistake is a mistake if only you don't learn from it."

***

"There is no shortcut. It takes time to build a better, stronger version of you."

***

"You've got to be a beginner before you can be anything else."

***

"Actually, the best gift you could have given her was a lifetime of adventure." Lewis Carroll 'Alice in Wonderland'

***

"Sometimes having coffee with a friend, is all the therapy you need."

***

"Road rage—small mind in big traffic,"

***

"Trust me, it matters."

***

"Style, class and patience 3 things you all have to work at."

***

"Be a scholar of life, learn all you can."

***

"When something is right, how can it be a waste of time?"

***

"Everyone has a fashion sense, some are more conscious of it."

***

"Grandparents are living history books."

***

"Justus is supposed to be blind, not deaf and dumb."

***

"If you give a man your heart, expect some wear and tear."

***

"When men get scared they leave—when woman get scared they shop."

***

"Children step on your hands when they are little and your heart when they are adults."

***

"Best friends are not above or below you, just beside you."

***

"Water seeks its own level."

***

"No matter how big a hammer you use, you can't pound common sense into stupid people."

***

"I desire stars. Why do I only yearn for what is out of reach?"

***

"Never put money in metal, put it in the ground and watch it grow."

***

"F.E.A.R has two meanings:

Forget Everything And Run

-or-

Face Everything And Rise

The choice is yours."

***

"Your only true legacy is your reputation."

***

"When the devil keeps asking you to look at your past, there must be something good in the future he doesn't want you to see."

***

"You will never have to force anything that is truly meant to be."

***

"People leave when it's their time to go, not yours."

***

"The ego wants quantity—the soul wants quality."

***

"Being rich has nothing to do with money."

***

"No one ever wins in war."

***

"God's plan for us is Peace, not Disaster."

***

"People change for two main reasons:
their minds have been opened,
or their hearts have been broken."

***

Chapter 8. The Holidays

When the winds turn cold and the house smells of cookies baking, the holidays are upon us, there's no mistaken. The family arrives as the food covers the table, but who am I kidding, its family, not a fable. The holidays we hope are full of good cheer, but when all else fails—grab the boys a beer. I'm usually cooking like a hired hand, so pass me some Whiskey of any brand. The cabinets are stocked, the wine has been poured, thank heaven for Canadian Club I've got something to look toward. So remember my friends when the holidays come to town, don't lose you head, don't let them get you down. Johnnie Walker and Jack Daniels will aid and assist, and don't forget Jim Bean, who could resist. The three wise men full of hope and praise will get you through, these blasted holidays.

****

"New Year's Eve is nothing more than armature night."

***

"Jack Frost nipping at your nose—they got a cream for that."

***

"I can't afford a vacation. So I'm just going to drink until I don't know where I am."

***

"Hot cocoa and fuzzy socks,"

***

"It wouldn't be Christmas without you."

***

"What kind of music did the Pilgrims like—Plymouth Rock,"

***

"Wishing you a season of gladness, a season of cheer and to top it all off—a wonderful New Year,"

***

"I'm dreaming of a white Christmas, but if the white runs out—I'll drink the red."

***

"Merry everything and happy always,"

***

"The holiday cheer will disappear."

***

"What does Tarzan sing at Christmas—JUNGLE BELLS,"

***

"Why did the turkey join the band—
because he had drumsticks,"

***

"What Christmas carol is sung in the desert—
a camel Ye Faithful."

***

"What's the best Christmas present in the world—
a broken drum, you just can't beat it."

***

"Let the evening be GIN-ger-ly"

***

"Wine will be my Valentine."

***

"Beer works better than mistletoe"

***

"May your life be like good wine, tasty, sharp and clear. And
like good wine may it improve with every passing year. An
Italian blessing,"

***

"What happens under the mistletoe stays under the mistletoe."

***

"As a child my family's meal time menus had two choices—
take it or leave it."

***

"Blood makes you related—loyalty makes you family."

***

"There are two way of arguing with Italian woman—neither
one works."

***

"Swear Jar—my swear jar could finance the fucking space
program."

***

"Tears, booze, I love the holidays too." Karen Walker

***

"This summer I need Vitamin Sea."

***

"Shot my first turkey today, scared the hell out of everyone in
the frozen food section."

***

"Drunk Uncle: 'To our wives and girlfriend, may they never
meet'."

***

"I don't need a Valentine, I need Valentino."

***

"Aunt Rosie: 'If you mated a Bulldog and A Shih Tzu would it be called Bullshit?'"

***

"Santa Clause has the right idea visit people only once a year."

***

"To say is to exist, to travel is to live."

***

"Almost everything will work again if you just unplug it for a few minutes—even you."

***

"I really can't stay, but baby its cold outside."

***

"What are you doing New Years, New Year's Eve?"

***

"When Black cats prowl and pumpkins gleam, may luck be yours on Halloween."

***

"May our sons have rich fathers and beautiful mothers?"

***

"Maybe Christmas, he thought, doesn't come from a store. Maybe Christmas perhaps means a little bit more." The Grinch

***

"The best way to spread Christmas cheer is singing loud for all to hear." ELF

***

"Merry Christmas, ya filthy animal" Home Alone

***

"Let's be naughty and save Santa the trip"

***

"Liquor makes people less boring around the holidays since about the 15th century."

***

"If kisses were snowflakes I'd send you a blizzard."

***

"It's a marshmallow world in the winter when the snow comes to cover the ground." Johnny Mathis

***

"Sure I drink more water around the holidays, granted it's frozen and surrounded by alcohol."

***

"Have a holy jolly Christmas" Burl Ives

***

"Let it snow, let it snow, let it snow..." Michael Buble

***

"Sweet, but twisted; does that make me a CANDYCANE?"

***

"It's the most wonderful time of the year, said no one who had to cook a ten course meal."

***

"I like thanksgiving turkey, it's the only time in Los Angeles you see natural breast." Arnold Schwarzenegger

***

"Thanksgiving is all about getting your whole dysfunctional family under one roof and praying the cops don't show up."

***

"I couldn't decide what to get you for Valentine's Day so I've decided to just get you NAKED."

***

"Just stole Santa's 'Naughty List', ironically it's almost identical to my friends list,"

***

"We are truly thankful that we won't have to see one another till next year."

***

"Santa saw your Instagram pictures; you're getting clothes and a bible."

***

"People who save room for pie 12%. Those who just loosen their pants 88%,"

***

"Can I just go 'trick or treating' and ask for wine?"

***

"The day after thanksgiving is the busiest day for plumbers."

***

"Christmas is so much worse when you get older. What do you want this year? I don't know, financial security, a career, a sense of purpose, fuck even a nap would be great."

***

"It's not important that you buy today, but you return tomorrow."

***

"Oh the weather outside can bite me, and my car won't start to spite me. And I can't feel any of my toes. WINTER BLOWS. WINTER BLOWS. WINTER BLOWS."

***

"I'll tell ya one thing—the tree isn't the only thing getting lit this year."

***

"Don't get your tinsel in a tangle."

***

"Be it ever so humble there's no place like home—except the holidays."

***

"Today I'm thankful for adult beverages."

***

"IF ifs and buts were beer and nuts, we'd all have a Merry Christmas" Erika Heinz

***

"May your stuffing be tasty, may your turkey be plump, may your potatoes and gravy have nary a lump. May your yams be delicious, may your pies take the prize, and may your THANKSGIVING DINNER stay off your thighs."

***

"Is it true that you just love me for my breast? A turkey wants to know."

***

"What did the pumpkin say to the turkey, 'laugh it up big shot you're up next.'"

***

"Eat, drink and wear stretchy-pants."

***

"The most important cooking instruction on thanksgiving is to add wine to the COOK."

***

"St. Nick arrives on Christmas Eve, in our house St. Nick arrived a bit early, December 21st we named him Nicholas."

***

"Emmanuel-God is with us."

***

"Gobble till you wobble."

**

"Al Capone, now he knows how to celebrate Valentine's Day."

***

"Dear Santa, I've been good all year. Most of the time, once in a while. Or forget it I'll buy my own stuff."

***

"Easter reminds us all why we are here on Earth."

***

"Family comes first, money is never top priority."

***

"I miss you most at Christmas Time." Mariah Carey

***

"Hey Santa, just leave your credit card under my tree."

***

"What am I getting for Christmas you ask—Drunk, I'm getting fucking drunk,"

***

"Relax, unwind, and get in a flip-flop state of mind."

***

"Let the Holidays be-GIN."

***

"Travel is the only thing you buy that makes you richer."

***

"Tis the season to be naughty,"

***

"Christmas is the only time of year you sit around a dead tree and eat candy out of old socks."

***

"Dear Santa, before I explain, how much do you know already?"

***

"This is New Year's Eve 3rd time this week"

***

"Make everyday a holiday, enjoy life."

***

"Most holidays have something to do with religion."

***

"Let there be peace on Earth, and let it begin with me."

***

"Dear Santa, this year I want a big fat bank account and a slim body. Please don't mix it up like you did last year."

***

"When Santa squeezes his fat white ass down the chimney tonight he's gonna find the jolliest bunch of assholes this side of the nuthouse." Christmas Vacations.

***

"Christmas has been cancelled apparently you told Santa you were good and he died laughing."

***

"What did the GINGERBREAD man put on his bed—a cookie sheet."

***

"Halloween the only day you can be whoever you want to be."

***

"Bang—what was that, someone shot Santa, he isn't coming this year."

***

"May you never be too grown up to search the skies on Christmas Eve."

***

♫"When the bells all ring and the horns all blow
And the couples we know are fondly kissing
Will I be with you or will I be among the missing?

Maybe it's much too early in the game
Oh, but I thought I'd ask you just the same
What are you doing New Year's?
New Year's eve?

Wonder whose arms will hold you good and tight
When it's exactly twelve o'clock that night
Welcoming in the New Year
New Year's eve

Maybe I'm crazy to suppose
I'd ever be the one you chose
Out of a thousand invitations
You received

Oh, but in case I stand one little chance
Here comes the jackpot question in advance
What are you doing New Year's?
New Year's Eve?

Oh, but in case I stand one little chance
Here comes the jackpot question in advance
What are you doing New Year's?
New Year's Eve?"♪

Bobby Caldwell

Chapter 9. Amusing, Hilarious and ostentatious

Amusing people are one of a kind, their funny, and cheerful most of the time. Hilarious people show up on the scene, they don't think their funny, you know what I mean. Friends tell jokes, bartenders too; I hope you enjoy what I've gathered for you. Laughter comes in many forms, take it from me, they'll help you weather the storms.

****

"I can run entirely on CAFFINE, SARCASM and inappropriate thoughts."

***

"Dear Algebra, please stop asking us to find you 'X'. She's never coming back and don't ask 'Y'."

***

"Two blondes were driving to Disneyland. The sign read: Disneyland Left—so they started crying and headed home."

***

"To be old and wise, you must first be young and stupid."

***

"I'm not arguing, I'm simply explaining why I'm right."

***

"Mexican word of the day: habanero—
I was gonna go bow hunting but I didn't HABANERO."

***

"Anger Management—mind over matter and my hands over
my mouth."

***

"If you don't like it here, there's 49 other states pick one." Ma

***

"If you're not coffee, chocolate or bacon, I don't need your
negativity today."

***

"When is this 'old enough to know better' supposed to kick
in?"

***

"My bank account is a constant reminder that I'm safe from
identity theft."

***

"I don't know how to act my age, I've never been this age
before."

***

"My wife Mary and I have been married for forty-seven years and not once have we had an argument serious enough to consider Divorce. Murder, yes, but Divorce, never."

***

"Husband and wife had a fight. Wife called her mom and said: 'I am coming to live with you.' Mom said, 'No darling, he must pay for his mistake. I am coming to live with you!'"

***

"If con is the opposite of pro, is congress the opposite of Progress?"

***

"If flying is so safe why do they call the airport the TERMINAL?"

***

"I don't jog because I've watched enough Law & Order to know that's how you end up finding a dead body."

***

"Wednesday, it's like the middle finger of the week."

***

"You attract what you fear. Oh my gawd, I'm so scared of $10 billion dollars."

***

"Life is all about ASS: you're either covering it, laughing it off, kicking it, kissing it, busting it, or trying to get a piece of it."

***

"Mexican word of the day: deliver
the doctor told me if I don't quit drinking the tequila
I'm gonna really hurt DELIVER."

***

"Respect is taught at home. If your kid is a disrespectful little
shit. It's your fault. Not society. Not music. Not video games.
YOURS." George Carlin

***

"Hey Walmart, if I wanted to check myself out, I'd stay at
home and shop Amazon," hire some more cashiers.

***

"Friendships go together like chips-n-salsa."

***

"A REDHEAD tells her BLONDE stepsister, 'I slept with a
Brazilian…' the BLONDE replies, 'Oh my God! You slut!
How many is a Brazilian?' "

***

"You can be mature and respectful and still have a dirty sense
of humor."

***

"Henry VIII slept with a giant Axe beside him,"

***

"Mexican word of the day: Cologne –I asked my brother if he
COLOGNE some money to me."

***

"You can curse a lot and still be highly intelligent with a tremendous vocabulary."

***

"Whoever said money can't buy happiness—didn't know where to shop."

***

"Baby I love every bone in your body especially mine."

***

"No I checked my receipt. I didn't buy any of your Bullshit today."

***

"I grew up with liquor and chocolate."

***

"Mexican word of the day: Frito-Lay—I love when my wife leaves the house, I'm FRITOLAY around and do nothing."

***

"It's Monday, I don't need an inspirational quote to start my day, just spike the coffee and shut the fuck up."

***

"Italian Problems: when people stare at you like you're crazy for pronouncing Ricotta and Mozzarella the correct way."

***

"Why did the Mexican take Xanax? For Hispanic attacks."

***

"Why aren't iPhone chargers called apple juice?"

***

"I don't care what you think about me, I don't think about you at all." Coco Chanel

***

"I need a hug or a CHANEL bag."

***

"The less people you chill with, the less bullshit you deal with."

***

"It takes 7 seconds for food to pass from your mouth to stomach. A human hair can hold 3kg. The length of a penis is three times the length of the thumb. The femur is as hard as concrete. A woman's heart beats faster than a man. Women blink 2 times as much as men. We use 300 muscles just to keep our balance when we stand. A woman has read this entire text. A man is still looking at his thumb."

***

"I typed 'BITCH' into my GPS and low and behold—I'm in your driveway."

***

"Mexican word of the day Horizon—I told my girl to stop texting and to keep HERIZON the road when she's driving."

***

"It takes many nails to build a crib, but only one screw to fill it."

***

"Mexican word of the day bodywash—did the CAVS win today? Who knows—no bodywash."

***

"A little boy killed a butterfly. Dad said 'No butter for two weeks.' The little boy killed a honey bee, the Dad said. 'No honey for two weeks'. Mom killed a cockroach. The little boy turns to his Dad and says, 'Are you gonna tell her, or should I do it?'"

***

"Is it rude to look at someone and start singing 'If you only had a brain?'"

***

"Wife: 'I think my mind is almost gone.' Husband: 'I'm not surprised you've been giving me a piece of it every day for years.' "

***

"I hate tacos—said no Juan ever."

***

"Most women are afraid of clowns, but somehow still date them."

***

"Friends are like snowflakes—if you pee on them they will go away."

***

"Mexican word of the day LESBIAN: 'I told my friends, lesbian our best behavior and maybe our wives will let us go drink.'"

***

"Mexican word of the day REPERCUSSIONS 'I farted so hard on my girlfriends couch, I REPERCUSSIONS'"

***

"I'm really into Crossfit. I cross my fingers and hope I can fit my ass in those jeans."

***

"When in Rome, do as many Romans as you can."

***

"I love you with all my boobs, I would say heart, but my boobs are bigger."

***

"Once I get what I want. I don't want it anymore."

***

"Dinosaurs are extinct—marriage is still around."

***

"My mother is a travel agent for GUILT TRIPS."

***

"Who ordered the extra large bowl of Trouble?"

***

"I went from watching the Soaps to living one."

***

"If this is love—I don't want it."

***

"I love my life, without you in it."

***

"You want to be friends. Sorry I'm not accepting applications at this time."

***

"Husbands are proof women have a sense of humor."

***

"Blondes tease, brunettes please."

***

"Men don't care what you do, until you do it."

***

"Where have all the great men gone?"

***

"Trust me—you're wrong."

***

"Sometimes nice isn't a good thing."

***

"Are you working hard, or hardly working?"

***

"She fell from the ugly tree and hit every branch on the way down."

***

"Duty is just a way of letting you know when you're in the shit."

***

"If I could rearrange the alphabet I would put 'U' and 'I' together."

***

"As the fish on the wall said—if I would have kept my mouth shut, I wouldn't be in this position."

***

"If she eats her French fires with a fork, she's probably not going to do that thing you like."

***

"If someone won't lift a finger to call you, to see you, to spend time with you. It's time for you to lift 5 fingers and wave goodbye."

***

"What hair color does your license read if you're bald?"

***

"Why do we need reality TV, isn't reality bad enough?"

***

"Never forget who ignored you when you needed them and who helped you before you even had to ask."

***

"Why do they sterilize the needle for Lethal Injections?"

***

"Why are there interstates in Hawaii?"

***

"If they squeeze olives to get olive oil, how the hell do they get baby oil?"

***

"Why is there Braille on a drive up ATM keypad?"

***

"Bumper sticker on a hearse… Have a Happy FOREVER."

***

"Las Vegas—a sunny place for shady people."

***

"A good driver is one who obeys the traffic laws and dodges those who don't."

***

"My days are numbered and my ship is late."

***

"Central Park, serenity in the middle of mayhem."

***

"Tipping is a matter of opinion; you just paid for the right to voice yours."

***

"The road to success is marked with many tempting parking places."

***

"If PSYCHIC's can see into the future why don't they buy a lottery ticket and really clean-up?"

***

"My mind works like lightening, one brilliant flash and it's gone."

***

"My family tree is full of NUTS."

***

"Little WHITE lies always lead to the case of the BLUES."

***

"You'll never respect someone who kisses your ass."

***

"If life is what you make of it—I've made a mess of mine."

***

"In every commercial break there is a car commercial followed by a food commercial, just put the damn car in the drive thru and be done with it."

***

"Hookers and Lawyers both screw people for money."

***

"In California I'm three hours younger."

***

"The law hasn't been on my side in a while."

***

"You went to Finishing-School—well to be honest, I had trouble finishing school."

***

"He told me like it is and I left him like he was nothing."

***

"Go People watching, its uninterrupted comedy."

***

"First comes the engagement ring, then the wedding ring, then the suffering."

***

"I'm off to save the world, Macys 50% off sale is today."

***

"The geek you made fun of in high school is now a computer genus."

***

"If there isn't POPCORN in heaven I'm out of there."

***

"Don't give up, remember Moses was a basket case."

***

"A good hairdresser holds your future in their hands."

***

"The object of my affection is in someone else's garage."

***

"The only birthdays that count are 1, 5, 10, 16, 18, 21, all others are just a reason to eat cake."

***

"The only light favored by women is a BUDLIGHT or CANDLE LIGHT."

***

"If love doesn't live here anymore—is the space available?"

***

"TIFFANY's can turn that frown upside down."

***

"WALMART, walls and walls of what's on the market,"

***

"Same old game, just different players."

***

"You must be delirious, cause you can't be serious."

***

"A man will sleep with a woman because of her exterior

A man will stick around because of her interior."

***

"The worst thing God did was give a man two heads, because they always think with the smaller one."

***

"The basic rate of speech is 140WPM, proves people talk too much."

***

"If Chocolate is the substitute for sex—there is no substitute for chocolate."

***

"My rainy day fund is bone dry."

***

"I had a problem my Godfather solution—cement shoes."

***

"This is a work site, if you don't work…get out of my sight."

***

"He may not be Fred Flintstone, but he made the bed-rock."

***

"Cellphones allow us to communicate with those individuals we would never call."

***

"I think the plate in your head is cracked."

***

"A pretty face gets old, a nice body will change, but a good woman will always be a good woman."

***

"She's like a doorknob, every guy took a turn."

***

"He's like railroad tracks, laid all over the county."

***

"I don't mean to toot my own horn but—BEEP, BEEP"

***

"People that leave a bad taste in your mouth will always find you."

***

"Money can't buy you love or happiness, but it can pay the rent."

"Mexican word of the day bishop—it wasn't until I gave my wife the credit card that I could shut the BISHOP."

***

"He asked me why the house isn't clean because I'm home all day. I asked him why we aren't rich since he works all day."

***

"I've dined in London, made love in Paris, and fought bulls in Spain—that's nothing I've been to Walmart on Black-Friday."

***

"I miss you like an idiot misses the point."

***

"Your face isn't a coloring book—chill out with the makeup."

***

"When life gives you lemons—freeze them and throw them as hard as you can at the people making your life difficult."

***

"Brains aren't anything—in your case they're nothing."

***

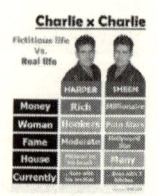

Chapter 10. Batman, the Joker & Society in General

Cleveland and Superheroes go hand and hand, remember my friends this is where it all began. Movies are filmed here, like The Avengers you see, but did you know—Superman was created here, in 1933? Two Jewish kids from Glenville High School Jerry Siegel and Joe Shuster created a comic mega-blockbuster. I grew up watching 'Batman' every chance I got; he was crafty and smart with a cast full of tarts. A fan of all 'super heroes' I must make my confession, I graduated from Glenville, back in the class of 1987.

"When people ask; 'what do you do?'
Answer; 'Whatever it takes."

"Can money buy happiness? Hell I'm willing to give it a shot."

"The only people I owe my loyalty to—those who never made me question theirs."

"The difference between you and I—
the RITZ is not just a cracker."

"I'm not your guidance counselor, or your conscious."

"The loudest one in the room is the weakest one in the room."

"Most of us won't be content with our lot until it's a lot-more."

"When I lost my excuses, I found my results."

"Beware of people who are in your Circle,
but not in your Corner."

"Age is just a number and mine is unlisted."

"A banker lends you an umbrella when it's sunny and asks for
it back when it's raining."

"When in doubt, remember F.I.S.H"
FUCK IT, SHIT HAPPENS

"I love this neighborhood; these broads are wearing my salary."

"Never open your mouth unless you in the dentist chair."
Sammy the bull Gravano

"Pay close attention to people who don't clap when you win,"

"The older you get, the more important it is to not act your age." Jack Nicholson

"A man is only as faithful as his options."

"If you have one year to live move next to me—every day feels like a fuckin eternity."

"Snitches get stitches."

"A bottle of scotch a couple of Aleve and I'm ready for anything."

"Wealth is not about having a lot of money—it's about having a lot of options." Chris Rock

"With a song in my heart and your hand over my mouth I can get through anything."

"It's okay if people don't like you. Most people don't even like themselves." Jack Nicholson

"Never forget 3 types of people in our life: 1. Who helped you in difficult times. 2. Who left you in difficult times. 3. Who put you in difficult times."

"The only respect that matters is self-respect." Rocky

"Success is usually the culmination of controlling failure." Sylvester Stallone

"Our greatest glory is not in falling, but the rising every time we fall." Rocky

"Don't let anyone get comfortable—disrespecting you."

"I say what the fuck needs to be said—not what you want to hear." The Joker

"In a world full of princesses, dare to be BATMAN"

"Patience: what you have when there are too many witnesses."

"He who is deaf, blind and silent lives a thousand years in Peace," John Gotti

"Madness as you know is a lot like gravity, all it takes is a little push." The Joker

"Not everyone gets the same version of me. One person might tell you I'm an amazing beautiful soul. Another person will say I'm a cold hearted bitch. Believe them both—I act accordingly."

"Commonsense is like deodorant, the people who need it most never use it."

"Love is grand; divorce is a hundred-grand."

"I was married by a judge, I should have asked for a Jury," Groucho Marx

"The less you give a fuck, the happier you'll be."

"If someone hates you for no reason—give the jerk a reason."

"Don't ever assume:
all you're doing in making an **ASS** out of **U** and **ME**."

"Never ruin an apology with an excuse,"

"Excuses are like assholes—everybody's got one."

"Actions speak louder than words, so believe what you see and fuck what you heard."

"Never rub another man's rhubarb." The Joker

"Sell crazy someplace else, we're all stocked up here." Jack Nicholson

"If you're good at something never do it for free." The Joker

"You either die a hero or you live long enough to see yourself become the villain." The Dark Knight

"If they want to see crazy—show it to them."

"The greatest prison people live in is the fear of what other people think." The Joker

"There are three types people in the world; Watchers, talkers, and doers."

"Never let the same person waste your time."

"Goals so big—you get uncomfortable telling small minded people."

"I heard you're a PLAYER, nice to meet you, I'm the COACH."

"Who gives a damn—when moneys on the table my friend."

"I don't trust words, I even question actions, but I never doubt patterns." The Godfather

"Whatever comes, comes whatever goes, goes—see what remains."

"Your heart knows the way, run in that direction."

"Stop being a push over and—push on,"

"You want to be taken seriously, stop dressing like a little girl."

"You weren't meant to understand
you just should have known,"

"You live but once, you might as well be amusing."

"Paris got Fashion, we got Whiskey."

"If you find me offensive, I suggest you quit fucking find me."

"Do you think I do this for my own good?"

"You want to be remembered do it out loud; you wanna be
happy, do it for yourself."

"Lions, Tigers and Bears…oh my, the game is one."

"Dress like you are going to meet your worst enemy today"
Coco Chanel

"If you can't be better than your competition just dress better"
Anna Wintour editor of Vogue

"Keep your heels, head and standards high" Coco Chanel

"You can be a good person with a kind spirit and still tell
people to go fuck themselves when needed."

"The best things in life are free. The second-best is expensive."
Coco Chanel

"Don't let small minds convince you that your dreams are too
big."

"Start from nothing, stop for nothing."

"You get lucky when you work your ass off."

"You can't do epic shit with basic people."

"If your goals set you apart from the crowd, stay alone."

"IF hard times make you stronger, than I should be able to whip SUPERMAN'S ass by now."

"Reality is stranger than fiction."

"My momma ain't raised no dummies."

"Good sex just hides what's wrong in a bad relationship."

"Everyone has two sides of Good and Evil, how you treat me will determine which side you see."

"Some days it feels like all I'm doing is rearranging deck chairs on the TITANIC."

"Why worry about foolish people?"

"Holly Golightly was right, there's no place like TIFFANY's."

"IF Satan ever loses his hair, there will be Hell-toupee."

"Imposter Perfume, a nobody trying to be a somebody."

"You are such a SUCK-UP if you came with attachments I could toss the Hoover."

"If I'm here to amuse you, its gonna cost you a lot."

"Want a second income—spend less."

"Never explain, your friends don't need it and your enemies won't believe it."

"The first screw in the head that comes loose is the one that controls the tongue."

"You were warned once, next time I'm bringing out the big guns."

"Moms got C.R.S. can't remember shit."

"Michael Keaton said it best…'I'm BATMAN'"

"You talk more than a Senator."

"Do I look like I was born yesterday?"

"Double negative—no job and no money"

"My ass is on the line, No your ass is out of line."

"Why is it that everything that tastes so good is so bad?"

"My state of mind right now is none of your business."

"Words don't cut it, Show it!"

"I'm not a cocky son of a bitch; I'm a confident son of a bitch."

"What part of love thy neighbor don't you understand?"

"On the keyboard of life keep one finger on the 'escape key'."

"Life is what you make of it; you've made my life less than it was."

"If the Pilgrims left England because of BULLSHIT, why the hell did they bring it here?"

"If money isn't everything, try living without it."

"Want to go back in time turn on TVLAND, but live in the presence."

"Come to PLAY stay to WIN."

"Be a MEXI-CAN not a MENI-CAN'T."

"Does the fun ever START?"

"Ten seconds on the lips, a lifetime on the hips."

"Must be your lucky day, meeting me,"

"The 80's were tobacco, alcohol and cars."

"You maybe way too handsome for me, but I am way too Good for you."

"Economy is often defined as the reduction of someone else's salary."

"The art world is 90% hot air."

"Shop in the name of Love,"

"Do I look like I'm kidding?"

"Of course you can have Friday off, just don't bother to show up Monday morning."

"Good news spreads fast, bad news moves at the speed of light."

"When I'm with you, I don't like myself."

"Camping is for people who don't know where the RITZ is."

"Aside from being NUTS, what else is bothering you?"

"CRACKERS, BANANAS and NUTS. Its food that makes you crazy."

"A child's mind is like a blank canvas, create a masterpiece."

"Prejudice is a product of environment."

"Remember even the three stooges were banned."

"I didn't ask to be a princess…I was born this way."

"The few, the underpaid—TEACHERS,"

"I'm not a 100% sure, I'm 1000% POSITIVE."

"Send in the CLOWNS, I'm calling off work!"

"Do unto others before they do unto you."

"A friend is someone who thinks you are a good egg even if you're slightly CRACKED."

"Time is the real enemy."

"Children's minds are open…is yours?"

"The best things in life are on SALE."

"Samples are invitations to the unknown."

"If the Pen is mightier than the sward, I'm gonna need more ink."

"Forgive, Forget and Full speed ahead."

"The impossible dream has possibilities."

"A computer is only as smart as the person in front of it."

"I hit the lottery when I met you, and filed for bankruptcy when you left."

"Lighten-up, stay out of the sun,"

"Life gets easier, when you get the hang of it."

"I'm the meat in an idiot sandwich sometimes."

"It's cute, how stupid you are."

"Crazy doesn't even begin to cover it."

"Stress is when you wake up screaming than realize you haven't slept yet."

"On you Mark, Get set…GO AWAY."

"I've just haven't been the same since that house fell on my sister."

"I seem to identify with Dorothy—I only attract men who are cowards, have no heart and are in need of a brain."

"I may be left handed, but I'm always right."

"Forgive me Father for I have shopped…"

"5 our fathers and 10 Hail Macys,"

"I fish there for I Lie."

"Baroque is when you are of MONET."

"To shop or not to shop the answer lies in the wallet."

"Face it we all want to be superheroes."

"Not all superhero wear a cape, mine wore a CROSS."

"Where's BATMAN & ROBIN when you need them?"

"If I could, I would like to live in a hotel."

"Fill you Tummy up—not out."

"A diamond is FOREVER—a cubic zirconia is for Right NOW."

"Try not to judge, we're not in COURT."

"They asked John Gotti's wife 'what does your husband do for a living?' she stood up proudly and said; 'He provides.' Then she walked out of the courtroom."

Chapter 11. Words from the Unknown

There are some that leave us all too soon, never quite understanding their gloom. Then there are some who were thoughtful enough to share, a poem, a verse that filled the air. Finally, we come upon those who have left us a tiny cornerstone, for they are simply—the unknown.

****

"If you haven't been in my shoes, don't talk about me like they fit you."

***

"The same boiling water that softens potatoes hardens eggs. It's all about what you are made of—not your circumstances."

***

"The history of the world is written with food and wine."

***

"I can't get old—I have too many things to do today."

***

"Life is a gift, love is a present, and happiness is an option."

***

"Love is an emotion, hate is learned."

***

"Anyone who talks by the yard and thinks by the inch should be moved by the foot."

***

"If you are persistent you'll get it.
If you are consistent you'll keep it."

***

"What is the biggest room in the world—room for improvement."

***

"Where is the best place to hide anything—under someone's nose."

***

"A pessimist is an optimist with experience."

***

"Anyone can be a writer; it takes a soul to be a Poet."

***

"To do the right thing you must first know the difference."

***

"Misfortune comes on horseback and departs on foot."

***

"Consider how hard it is to change yourself and you'll understand what little chance you have in trying to change others."

***

"Don't be a pebble in anyone's shoe."

***

"Your vibe attacks your tribe."

***

"If you really want something you will find a way—if you don't you will find an excuse."

***

"She is clothed in strength and dignity and laughs without fear of the future."

***

"Beautiful faces are everywhere, but beautiful minds are hard to find."

***

"If you don't take care of your customers, someone else will."

***

"Happiness will never come to those who fail to appreciate what they already have."

***

"There are two reasons why we don't trust people, first—we don't know them. Secondly—we know them."

***

"Sometimes you have to forget what you feel and remember what you deserve."

***

"My soul is from elsewhere, I'm sure of that, and I intend to end up there."

***

"Coincidence is when God chooses to remain anonymous."

***

"It's not the minutes spent at the table that puts on weight— it's the seconds."

***

"Sometimes 'I love you' isn't enough."

***

"Doubt sees obstacles—faith sees ways."

***

"Don't wait for six strong men to take you to church."

***

"Those who anger you—control you."

***

"It's better to bite your tongue, rather than to have it bite someone else."

***

"Your cell already replaced your camera, your calendar, your alarm clock—don't let it replace your FAMILY."

***

"Sometimes the worst place you can be is in your own head."

***

"Should you ever find yourself the victim of other people's jealousy, lies and insecurities…don't be mad. Remember things could be worse: You could be them."

***

"The only time you should ever look back is too see how far you've come."

***

"Happy are they who still have hope."

***

"We all have a cross to bear."

***

"Happy are those who are poor in spirit, theirs is the kingdom of God."

***

"Restless is the heart."

***

"Do not think of me as gone, I'm with you in the dawn."

***

"Reputation is for the time, character is for eternity."

***

"Artificial Intelligence is no match for Natural Stupidity."

***

"If you must choose between two evils, pick the one you've never tried before."

***

"If ignorance is bliss why aren't there more happy people?"

***

"The hardest of all work is doing nothing."

***

"Most are better at broadcasting than listening."

***

"No one ever learned anything new by talking."

***

"A good idea never came from a swelled head."

***

"A Nurse has the touch of an Angels Wing."

***

"It's okay to want, just don't forget what's in your hand."

***

"Truth is an unpopular subject. Because it is unquestionably correct,"

***

"This is not a day to take risks. Diplomacy rules today."

***

"Brains are in the breeding."

***

"An eye for an eye will make the world blind."

***

"If yellow and blue make green, then Sunshine and Water make greenery."

***

"Vision: the ability to see beyond the obstacles."

***

"All it takes is all you got."

***

"Ordinary people are the seeds of excellence."

***

"Cater to children and your business with prosper."

***

"Good things come to those who wait, better things come to those who don't give up and the best things come to those who believe."

***

"The human mind is such a deranged masterpiece, for it allows us to fall back into the same things that will always hurt us."

***

"Every hour spent fishing adds an hour onto your life,"

***

"The world is a circle, are you on the straight and narrow, or the curve?"

***

♫ "The world is a circle without a beginning
And nobody knows where it really ends
Everything depends on where you
Are in the circle that never begins
Nobody knows where the circle ends,"♪

Chapter 12. Stuff Cabbage for the Heart

Chicken Soup might be Jewish Penicillin that cures the common cold, but in my family, Stuff Cabbage was the meal, so mighty and bold. Sunday dinner was never complete without stuff cabbage; you could smell it cooking down the street. It's a warm dish of comfort, on a cold winter's day that feeds the soul in its own special way. Stuff cabbage is that conundrum that reminds me simply—where we've come from.

****

"If it rains on your parade—bring an umbrella."

***

"Did you know? Every day the Catholic Church feeds, clothes, shelters and educates more people than any other organization in the world."

***

"No tears in the writer, no tears in the reader, no surprise in the writer, no surprise in the reader" Robert Frost

***

"It's more impressive to play the piano than to pick one up."

***

"If you give the DEVIL and inch he becomes your ruler."

***

"I used to believe friends were a gift, now I realize they can sometimes be a FRUITCAKE."

***

"Watch your step—all others do,"

***

"A bargain is something you don't need at a price you can't resist."

***

"Waking up in truth is so much better than living a lie." Idris Elba

***

"A brick makes a house; a family makes it a home."

***

"D.N.A. your history behind your smile,"

***

"You're getting so old; your back goes out more than you do."

***

"Who we are comes from our genes, what we are, is a product of environment."

***

"Financial ruin is not the worst thing that can happen—
spiritual loss is worse."

***

"A bicycle can't stand on its own because it's two-tired."

***

"Some people are like buttons they pop-off at the wrong time."

***

"The more you grow-up the less your blow-up."

***

"A good idea never came out of a swelled head."

***

"I thanked the Indians for the rain, the farmers for the grain and
Nabisco for the Oreos"

***

"Who can you turn to when the chips fall—
Snyder's and Frit-o-lay of course."

***

"If you're supposed to give till it hurts—
I've been in pain for years."

***

"Sometimes being too sweet you might wind up a sucker."

***

"12 things to always remember:
1.the past cannot be changed. 2. Opinions don't define your reality. 3. Everyone's journey is different. 4. Things always get better with time. 5. Judgments are a confession of character. 6. Overthinking will lead to sadness. 7. Happiness is found within. 8. Positive thoughts create positive things. 9. Smiles are contagious. 10. Kindness is free. 11. You only fail if you quit. 12. What goes around comes around."

***

"Friends go together like chips-n-salsa."

***

"My mother made me chicken, the chicken made me cough; maybe she should have taken all of the feathers off."

***

"I can explain it to you—but I can't understand it for you."

***

"Why live your life in Distress—when God wants your life to be blessed."

***

"When friends and money collides only one wins,"

***

"Never argue with someone who believes their own lies."

***

"I'm not upset that you lied to me, I'm upset that from now on I can't believe you." John Gotti

***

"Let's get one thing straight. I'm not yelling—I'm just Italian!"

***

"A man is the head of the family, but it's the woman who is the neck." My big fat Greek wedding

***

"The best inheritance parents can leave a child is a good name."

***

"Thinking well is wise, planning well is wiser, and doing well is wisest."

***

"Be content with your lot—ever satisfied with your achievements."

***

"I'm not the cause, I'm the effect."

***

"It's time to be the best instead of masquerading as the best."

***

"I need you to lead, follow or get fuck out of my way."

***

"When someone dies you don't lose them all at once, you lose them in pieces."

***

"Never underestimate the power of a good meal."

***

"A saint is a sinner who never stopped trying."

***

"How nice is it to find someone who asks for nothing but your company."

***

"Go for the GLORY, but keep your dignity."

***

"Comfort Food feeds the body and nourishes the soul."

***

"My one and only regret hasn't happened yet."

***

"Some people could see better in the day if they didn't run around at night."

***

"Live so that even the Funeral Director will be sorry when you die."

***

"After dad passed away we were blessed with his smile, we named her Autumn."

***

"Ethnic music touches the heart and soul in its own language."

***

"When you walk away, know you gave it your all, or it's really not over."

***

"You look good from afar, and far from GOOD."

***

"Please be patient before you become one."

***

"Sometimes small changes make big differences."

***

"No matter who you marry, you always wake-up with someone else."

***

"Grief is the price we pay for LOVE."

***

"'I can't' quickly translates to, 'I'm afraid to extend myself' "

***

"Whoever you hate, will wind up in your family."

***

"Self-confidence is the best accessory, oh and God, a Chanel bag doesn't hurt."

***

"The same man, who captured your heart, can also break it."

***

"I'm as nervous as a long tailed cat in a room full of rocking chairs."

***

"When you let CRAZY into your life, remember you must take the good and prepare for the BAD."

***

"When God closes a door, he opens a window—
why are there bars on mine?"

***

"As long as you can accept the consequences, your actions are altered."

***

"It doesn't matter where you grew-up—
how you were raised matters."

***

"Passion changes everything."

***

"Finding your passion isn't about careers and money. It's about finding your authentic self—the one you've buried beneath the needs of others."

***

"Those who can, do—those who can't teach."

***

"The only ones, who matter, are the ones we count on."

***

"You're a liar and a thief—I only lied about being a thief."

***

"Sometimes you have to FORGET what you feel and
REMEMBER what you deserve."

***

"No one ever said 'It drives like a Lincoln.' "

***

"WHY because I said so that's WHY."

***

"Kids are a blessing and a lesson, in all that there is to come."

***

"People like you are the reason people like me need
medication."

***

"Pretty little blue-eyed miss, full of charm and tenderness, I'd
love to give you a great big kiss." Joe Jeromos

***

"You lie and cheat on me, lie and cheat on me constantly, yes
sir-re, where were you last night until three—you were out

with someone new, while I stayed home, just waiting for you."
Autumn Lacey

***

"Darling I'm so drunk, just look at me, I've had a lot of beer and wine, it's plain to see, I can't get home dear, my legs won't carry me—so let me stay with you tonight how happy we would be."

***

"Teach the art of love to me tonight dear;
let me have some happiness at last."

***

"My sweetheart is a lovely little miss."

***

"Happy music Hungarian style, dance along with a great big smile, everybody's happy singing, everybody's swinging madly, come and sing along with me…"

***

"You just can't trust a redhead, beware of anything she said, after she caught you, she'll go after another, she'll go through life from lover to lover, you just can't trust a redhead."

***

"If you'll only say you'll marry me—
how happy you and I will be."

***

"If you'd ever leave darling, you'd cry alone, you'd kiss my
picture, and cry by the phone."

***

"Kiss me darling hold me tight, while the moon is bright, lets
enjoy each other's charms on this enchanting night—holding
you and kissing you fills me with ecstasy—oh promise me
you'll always stay in love with me."

***

♫ "Hello such a simple way to start a love affair
Should I jump right in and say how much I care
Would you take me for a mad man or a simple hearted clown
Hello with affection from a sentimental fool
To a little girl who's broken of every rule
One who brings me up when all the others seem to let me down
One whose nice to be around

Should I say that it's a blue world without you
Nice words I remember from an old love song
But all wrong, cause I never called it love before
This feeling's new - this came with you

And I know that the nicest things that never seem to last
That we're both a bit embarrassed by our past
But I think there's something special in the feelings that we've
found
And you're nice to be around." ♪

***

Chapter 13. You gotta friend in me

There are all sorts of pets that fill our home, from cats and rabbits, oh how they roam. The hamsters and frogs greet you every day, but I love the ducks as they waddle away. No one can resist a puppy or hound, and how could I forget Homeward Bound. The turtles are slow; the gerbils run fast, maybe that's why my dog just ran pass? The fish fill my tank, as they move all about; damn I forgot to take the trash out. What can I say, pets keep me hopping; some need litter and some need walking? Most need care and shelter after all. Perhaps a few toys, damn! I stepped on one in the hall. Pets need food, water and such. Ferrets and pigs I can't get enough. Parrots and bugs can teach you a lot, but if you really want to learn, give crabs and lizards a shot. I'll end with the horses that can carry you away, when a giant scary spider, gets in your way. Oh there are all sorts of pets.

****

"My Dogs favorite bone is in my Postman's leg."

***

"Our prime purpose in this life is to help others, and if you can't help them at least don't hurt them."

***

"Scooby-Doo taught us that in the end the real monsters were always HUMAN."

***

"I distrust Camels or anyone else who can go a whole week without a drink." Joe E. Lewis

***

"The only honest ones at the racetrack are the horses."

***

"Some of my best leading men were dogs and horses"
Elizabeth Taylor

***

"God gave us dogs so when things are backwards we'll always know he is there."

***

"Does honey make you pee—it made Winnie POO."

***

"My horse came in so late they paid the jockey time and a half."

***

"Men are like dogs—when you stop chasing them, they'll start chasing you."

***

"A home without a dog is like a garden without any flowers."

***

"Be kind to ever kind"

***

"I must be a mermaid; I have no fear of depths, and a great fear of shallow living."

***

"It's not the size of the dog in the fight; it's the size of the fight in the dog."

***

"What's the difference between bird flu and swine flu? One requires tweetment and the other requires oinkment."

***

"Dogs can't operate MRI machines…but Cats-scan"

***

"What do you call a camel with no hump—Humphrey,"

***

"Have you ever met someone so stupid that you felt bad for their dog?"

***

"I want a man who's loyal, faithful, patience, attentive, forgiving, unselfish, and even-tempered yet a good listener. Oh honey, you want a DOG."

***

"All Dogs go to heaven"

***

"Our little mini-pincher should be in Jail, cause it ought to be illegal to be this cute." Erika & Abriana

***

"Dogs are Gods way of apologizing for your relatives."

***

"If we all love as hard as dogs do,
the world would be a better place."

***

"The TROUT, the whole TROUT, and nothing but the TROUT so help me COD."

***

"Learn a lesson from your dog; no matter what life brings you—kick some dirt over that shit and move on."

***

"Happiness is when you look at your pet and forget all your problems."

***

"God spelled backwards is DOG."

***

"Milo and Otis the purr-fect odd couple"

***

"♫Soft kitty, warm kitty, little ball of fur. Happy kitty, sleepy kitty…purr…purr…purr…♪" The big bang theory

***

"Love is a four legged word."

***

"The road to my heart is paved with paw prints."

***

"♫Smelly cat, smelly cat, what are they feeding you? ♪" Friends

***

"Be the person your dog thinks you are."

***

"When all else fails—hug the dog."

***

"Best friends are ones with paws."

***

"Animals are sent by those who have died to let you know you're not alone."

***

"When a red Cardinal appears in your yard
it's a visitor from heaven."

***

"Feather stands for hope, balance and good luck."

***

"How you treat animals tells me all I need to know about you."

***

"When I needed a hand I found your paw."

***

"The best therapist has fur and four legs."

***

"Meow, meow, meow= I love you."

***

"Dogs do speak, but only to those who know how to listen."

***

"Did you know dogs can smell fear?"

***

"I feel sorry for people who don't have dogs, they have to pick
up food they drop."

***

"Animals let you be you."

***

"Licks on face, poop on the floor and treats all around."

***

"Bark, Bark, it's a Ruff world out there without a license."

***

"Hi there, can I spend my 9 lives with you."

***

"For the best seat in the house, you will have to move the dog."

***

"Of course ya can stay; there is always room for one more."

***

"Handle every situation like a dog, if you can't eat it, or play with it, just piss on it and move on."

***

"Can you tell me the story about how you rescued me again?"

***

"Oh you're allergic to cats—Good, I'm allergic to idiots."

***

"When the dog bites, when the bee stings, when I'm feeling sad—these are a few of my favorite things."

***

"Some people need a kiss—on the neck from a crocodile."

***

"Who let the dogs out—me,"

***

"Not a creature was stirring not even a mouse—cause I ate him." Cat of the house

***

"I would slap you but I don't want to get stupid on my paws,"

***

♫"You've got a friend in me
When the road looks, rough ahead
And you're miles and miles
From your nice warm bed
Just remember what your old pal said
Boy, you've got a friend in me

You've got a friend in me
You've got troubles, well I've got 'em too
There isn't anything I wouldn't do for you
We stick together and we see it through
You've got a friend in me."♪

Chapter 14. Proverbs

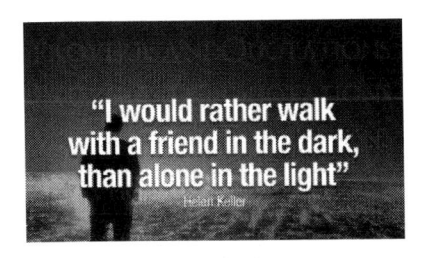

By definition a Proverb is a simple concrete saying that delivers a message most worthy of conveying. It holds popularity expressing a truth, from the mighty elders to today's frolicking youth. Based on common sense, some metaphorical, some based on fact, some even historical. However, almost every culture has a Proverb or two they share—here are few that fill the air.

****

"Find your God given talent—whatever you do down here, you'll do up there."

***

"Always on my mind, forever in my heart,"

***

"Don't trust what you see, even salt looks like sugar."

***

"He who plants kindness, reaps love."

***

"Penny wise and a dollar foolish,"

***

"A lie is proof of what is not true."

***

"Life is ironic, it takes sadness to know what happiness is, noise to appreciate silence, and absence to value presence."

***

"Life is about choices and living with the consequences."

***

"Peace follows pain, rebirth follows ruin."

***

"Credo *Imposible*—I believe the impossible."

***

"A kind word is like a spring day," Russian Proverb

***

"Lord if it's not your will, let it slip through my grasp and give me the peace not to worry about it."

***

"Tension is who you think you should be. Relaxation is who you are." Chinese proverb

***

"Faith is seeing light with your heart when all your eyes see in darkness."

***

"Stay where there are songs." Roma proverb

***

"The body heals with play, the mind heals with laughter, and the spirit heals with joy."

***

"Trust the one who can see 3 things in you: Sorrow behind your smile. Love behind your anger. Reason behind your silence,"

***

"According to Greek Mythology, humans were originally created with four arms, four legs and a head with two faces. Fearing their power, Zeus split them into two separate beings, condemning them to spend their lives in search of their other halves." Plato's The Symposium (Not my view, but I found it interesting,)

***

"Do not correct a fool or he will hate you. Correct a wise man and he will appreciate you."

***

"It's nice to be important, but more important to be nice."

***

"Arrogance is the camouflage of insecurity."

***

"The root of Suffering is attachment" Buddha

***

"Walk with the wise and become wise; associate with fools and get in trouble." Proverbs 13:20

***

"We live at the edge of Miraculous"

***

"Offer me something I cannot find in myself."

***

"They tried to bury us. They didn't know we were seeds."
Mexican proverb

***

"It does not matter how slow you go, as long as you do not stop." Confucius

***

"Do what is hard and your life will be easy. Do what is easy and your life will be hard."

***

"Do things that feed your soul, not your ego and you will be happy"

***

"To err is human—to forgive is divine."

***

"Keep Calm and Marry On"

***

"There are no foolish questions, only the one that is not asked"

***

"Read a thousand books and your words will flow like a river."

***

"Lonely for you—dear only"

***

"When someone you love becomes a memory, the memory becomes a treasure."

***

"The beginning of Wisdom is Silence, the second is listening."

***

"Courage doesn't mean you don't get afraid. Courage means you don't let fear stop you."

***

"Courage is the commitment to begin without any guarantee of success"

***

"To heal a wound you need to not touch it."

***

"Not all those who wander are lost"

***

"Regret nothing. Everything broken can be remade. And everything remade can once again be broken."

***

"Those who distrust most should be trusted least"

***

"Being positive in a negative situation is not naïve. It's leadership."

***

"If it doesn't open, it's not your door"

***

"We weave in time, what we wear in eternity."

***

"Every day needs a purpose."

***

"If you pray—it will happen"

***

"All good things must come to an end."

***

"Hope comes in many forms."

***

"Change is hard; some have to change from the outside in."

***

"A missed hello becomes the long GOOD-BYE."

***

"God has the power to show you who's GOD"

***

"I pray for you more than I pray for myself these days."

***

"Life rewards the courageous few."

***

"Be honest, not confrontational."

***

"Life reward, let courage flow."

***

"Time is a monster, you can't reason with it."

***

"Christ asks us to love both work and our enemies."

***

"I am blessed with work."

***

"Many things can give wisdom, but only love can make one wise."

***

"Be fishers of people, you catch them, God will clean them."

***

"It is wise to act wise, unless you're otherwise."

***

"The will of GOD will never take you to where the Grace of GOD will not protect you."

***

"The secret to living well and long is: eat half, walk double, laugh triple and love without measure." Tibetan Proverb

***

"Every shoe has a mate"

***

"Miracles happen when you replace tears with prayers and fear with FAITH."

***

"There's beauty in simplicity."

***

"Second thoughts are often wiser than first impressions."

***

"Only speak well of people and you'll never have to whisper."

***

"There is a difference between waiting and hoping."

***

"Respect the crown, but love the man."

***

"A man with no means, but has faith is already wealthy."

***

"Heavy is the head that wears the CROWN."

***

"If you don't try you'll never know."

***

"Failure is part of the learning process."

***

"God alone changes people, he does it all."

***

"Seeing someone else's Point of View is quite difficult."

***

"Marriage is about finding a middle ground."

***

"Your success lies not in a lack of ability, but in a lack of ambition."

***

"The 3 great healers: TIME, NATURE and PATIENCE."

***

"Only you can make your dreams a reality."

***

"Trying to perfect one-self can be never ending."

***

"If you've got it, be careful of who might see it."

***

"Violence is never the answer."

***

"The eyes are the windows to the soul."

***

"How much is too much?"

***

"The best way to get ahead in this world is to be born with one."

***

"Confidence is King."

***

"It only looks like a big effort, because you never made one before."

***

"It's never too late."

***

"10-Q—welcome"

***

"What's important to you?"

***

"Everyone wants to belong."

***

"Changing the label doesn't alter the contents of the bottle."

***

"8hours of work+ 8hours of Play+ 8hours of Sleep = A perfect day"

***

"WAR will happen; you have to work for PEACE."

***

"All inclusive excludes no-one."

***

"I thought blood was thicker than money."

***

"Thanks and praise doesn't cost a cent, but means a lot."

***

"The wage of sin is death, repent before payday."

***

"June is God's apology for January."

***

"True love is measured by a thermometer of sacrifices."

***

"The fragrance of springtime is JESUS."

***

"A Stubborn person is hard to move."

***

"Educate yourself it will pay off."

***

"Friendships need friction to make them stronger."

***

"First impressions last forever."

***

"A self-made person must be careful they are not a good
example of unskilled labor."

***

"The poorest man in the world is richer than we know."

***

"Families should grow together, not apart."

***

"Don't lose sight of ones closest to you."

***

"A well beaten path is not necessarily the right way."

***

"Whenever I lose my sight on what's important, I look around and count my blessings."

***

"So it shall be written, so it shall be told."

***

"Don't make comedy out of someone else's tragedy."

***

"When you give, you truly receive."

***

"Art is a matter of opinion."

***

"Choose your battles wisely."

***

"If you hang out with dirt, you will become a weed."

***

"A fools name is seen in public."

***

"What's fair isn't always right."

***

"Time waits for no man."

***

"It's not the meaning of life, but the feeling of life."

***

"Breath it's the meaning of life"

***

"One's attitude is Tailor made."

***

"Wisdom is the key to all knowledge."

***

"Everything Must Change, nothing and no one remains the same."

***

"They say your conscious is God."

***

"If's it been handed down, it's bound to be around."

***

"Everything means nothing, if I don't have you."

***

"The spirit of poverty is having little and enjoying it."

***

"Correction does much, but encouragement does more."

***

"You do not believe what you don't live."

***

"Paying attention is money in the bank."

***

"The greatest remedies for anger are—delay."

***

"Tuition is expensive in the school of experience."

***

"Fame comes in many Venues."

***

"When the gray skies leave, will your attitude go with it?"

***

"Vision is more that the ability to see."

***

"A child once said, 'I'm here to save you.'"

***

"A quilt is a family of Stitches."

***

"Don't be someone's excuse, be someone's will."

***

"A pessimist is an optimist without any experience."

***

"A circle is the longest distance to the same point."

***

"Remember double negatives are a...no—no."

***

"Laugher is the shortest distance between two people."

***

"What happens when the money is no longer enough?"

***

"You are never too young to learn or educate."

***

"Smile and the whole world smiles back."

***

"When you're reaching for your future, why are you holding onto the past?"

***

"My tears have turned into time."

***

"M.A.B.L.E.—mothers always bring extra love."

***

"People, who have the least, give the most."

***

"Happy is the bride the sun shines on."

***

"A laugh a day keeps the doctor away."

***

"Today is a gift that is why it's called the Present."

***

"People lose their way when they lose their WHY."

***

"A big head is difficult to keep under ones hat."

***

"Patience is a great virtue, but work while you wait."

***

"Be Kind. Be Fair. Be honest. Be true, and all these things will come back to you."

***

"Even miracles take a little time" The Fairy Godmother

***

"Even a fish can avoid problems if it keeps its mouth shut."

***

"Here's to life and love and all that comes with it."

***

"Dare to be you,"

***

Five ethics of life:

LISTEN-before you speak

EARN-before you spend

THINK-before you write

TRY-before you quit

LIVE-before you die

***

"Old ways won't open new doors."

***

"Fools take knifes and stab people in the back.

The wise take the knife and cut the cord

freeing themselves from fools."

***

"Even a miracle needs a hand."

***

"The best seven doctors:

Sunshine, Air, Exercise, Water, Diet, Rest, and Laughter."

***

"Be stronger than your excuses."

***

"Anyone can find the dirt in some, be the one that finds the gold." Proverbs 11:27

***

"What is the difference between I like you and I love you?"

Beautifully answered by Buddha:

'When you like a flower you just pick it.

When you love a flower you water it daily.'

***

"I never said I was a saint,"

***

"Money has nothing to do with raising loving children."

***

Chapter 15. Limericks and all things Irish

Growing up in Ohio is a joy like no other, we all attend Mass just like me mother. An Irish Catholic Church so mighty and bold, we studied our Catechism and every Saints to behold. I'm quite fond of the Irish, a right mighty bunch, who would had known I'd love them so much. So funny and clever they're one of a kind, such down hearted people you'll ever find. Irish food is a comfort that just warms my heart, from the corned beef and cabbage, oh God where do I start? They're fond of the drink from time to time, but heaven knows, I surly don't mind. From stories that linger to drinks that never end, it's just the Irish way—my we little friend.

And to my dear Irish friend whom I've come to adore, you are blessings and wishes that I always look for. Being Irish by association is better than none; you still enjoy the Craic while ya have another one. Annie Dunne I miss ya more each day, meet me for a pint—what'ya say.

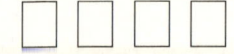

"When it rains at a funeral the heavens open ta welcome ya in"

"To friends who are caring and never do part, you'll always have a place right here in me heart."

"Here's to staying positive and staying negative."

"To absent friends…hip, hip hooray"

"Never complain, Never Explain."

"Blessed be those who have seen us at our best and seen us at our worst and can't tell the difference."

"Don't piss on my leg and tell it's raining."

"The best thing to hold onto in life is each other."

"Here's to a long life and a happy one, a quick death and an easy one, a good girl and an honest one, a cold pint and another one."

"A birthday blessing: may you be poor in misfortune, rich in blessings. Slow to make enemies, quick to make friends. But rich or poor, quick or slow, may you know nothing but happiness from this day forward,"

"May you be in heaven half an hour before the devil knows you're dead,"

"Paddy takes his son to the zoo: when they get to the elephants the zoo keeper said. 'This elephant can tell your age with just one look.' Paddy's son yelled 'How old am I?' The elephant stamps his foot 6 times. 'Wow' says Paddy confirming his boy is 6 years old. Paddy shouts to the elephant 'How old am I.' The elephant farts and stamps his foot twice. 'Bejesus!' says Paddy 'He's right I'm Farty-Two!!'"

***

"Oh fer feck sake… I'm not yelling…I'm Irish, we just live loud!"

"People worry if the glass is half empty or half full, they're missing the points it's refillable."

"You know you were raised by Irish parents, if in any crisis large or small the first thing to say is Jesus, Mary and Joseph."

"Everybody can't be Irish, someone has to drive."

"That which does not kill me, had better run."

"'O'feck it', sometimes that's all ye can say,"

"I'm sick of all the Irish stereotypes, as soon as I finish this beer I'm punching someone."

"If you love Irish guys raise your hands, if you don't, raise your standards."

"Being a bit Irish we don't tan, our freckles will connect."

"'A whiskey please,' 'Sir this is McDonalds' 'Okay make it a Mc-Whiskey, please.'"

"May the strength of God pilot us, May the wisdom of God instruct us, May the hand of God protect us. May the word of God direct us,"

"When you are Irish you know your problems can be solved by tea, holy water or Jameson and Guinness."

"A drunk goes to court. The judge says 'You've been brought here for drinking.' The drunk replies 'Great, let's get started.' "

"I don't even believe myself when I say I'm only gonna have."
one.

"Many a time, a man's mouth, broke his nose."

"Pubs, the official sunblock of Ireland"

"How to speak Irish: Wale, Oil, Beef, Hooked
(say really fast.)"

"Faith is like driving in the fog."

"Kilt: because balls like these don't fit in trousers."

"The Irish fight amongst themselves
because they yet to find a worthy opponent."

"Irish diet tip, your pants will never be too tight, if you never wear any."

"A boy may kiss his girl goodbye, the sun may kiss the butterfly, the wine may kiss the crystal glass and you my friend may kiss my ass."

"Irish advice: never approach a bull from the front, a horse from the rear or an idiot from any direction."

"Women are made to be loved, not understood" Oscar Wilde

"If the marriage isn't good from the get go.
Ya best be going on your way."

"Irish women are like teabags, they don't know their own true strength until they're in hot water."

"As you slide down the banister of life, may the splinters never point in the wrong direction,"

"Tis easy enough to be pleasant, when life hums along like a song, but the man worthwhile, is the man who can smile, when everything goes dead wrong."

"Get rich quicker, count your blessings."

"My mom has a gift for the gab; you my friend have a gift for swearing."

"May you never steal, lie or cheat, but if you must steal, then steal away my sorrow, if you must lie, then lie with me all the nights of my life and if you must cheat, then cheat death, because I could never live a day without you" an Irish blessing.

"I had the right to remain silent, but being Irish I didn't have the ability."

"May you have warm words on a cold evening, a full moon on a dark night and a smooth path to your door,"

"Being Irish you know that a good funeral is better than a bad wedding."

"May the hinges of our friendship never grow rusty."

"Wife: 'look at that drunken guy.' Husband: 'Who is he?' Wife: 'Ten years back he proposed to me and I rejected him.' Husband: 'Oh my God, he's still celebrating.'"

"How many beans did ya put in the pot Annie? Two hundred and Thirty-nine, if I added one more it would be TWO…FARTY."

"The Iris Way: now don't be talking about yourself while you're here, we'll surely be doing that once you leave."

"May the Irish hills caress you, may her lakes and rivers bless you, may the luck of the Irish enfold you. May the blessings of St. Patrick behold you."

"When Irish eyes are smiling they're usually up ta something."

"Erin go Bragh-less"

"If you were born without wings, don't hinder them from growing."

"Some people are like buttons, they POP-OFF at the wrong time."

"Be what you want to be, but remember who you are."

"If Age is not important, then why keep track?"

❧❧❧

"Irish Curse: May your mother in law move in with you."

❧❧❧

"The biggest part of judging character, is knowing yourself."

❧❧❧

"May the happiest day of your past,
be your saddest day of your future."

❧❧❧

"Growing old is inevitable-growing-up is optional."

❧❧❧

"People grow old when they quit playing."

❧❧❧

"After how far we've come, war is still not the answer."

❧❧❧

"Why is forgetfulness a familiarity?"

❧❧❧

"If God excludes no one, who are you to?"

❧❧❧

"Silence is often misinterpreted, but never miss-quoted."

❧❧❧

"Why look for a perfect church, you'd be out of place."

"Mother Nature never goes out of style."

"Nothing matters more than family."

"I'm always my worst critic."

"When my time comes, will I be ready?"

"Be a believer."

"Never let your guard down."

"To get through life, you must first have one."

"Most women start with an hourglass figure,
then over time the sand shifts."

"Think beyond your natural ability, you'll be surprised."

"Mental housekeeping keeps ya focused."

"Life is like a board game; just don't lose all your pieces."

"Dreamers have no boundaries."

"If mom was blessed with me, why was I cursed with you?"

"My time is a terrible thing to waste."

"Life is like a jigsaw puzzle,
every piece is part of the big picture."

"There's no such thing as just one lie."

"When it comes to family, it all matters."

"The Grass is always greener…in IRELAND."

"You can take my possessions, but you can't have my pride."

"Time is money, wasted, borrowed or spent."

"It just feels better if you get it on sale"

"Good girls are made of sugar and spice; Irish girls are made of Jameson on ice."

♫"Oh, Danny boy, the pipes, the pipes are calling
From glen to glen, and down the mountain side.
The summer's gone, and all the roses falling,
It's you, it's you must go and I must bide.

But come ye back when summer's in the meadow,
Or when the valley's hushed and white with snow,
It's I'll be here in sunshine or in shadow,
Oh, Danny boy, oh Danny boy, I love you so!

But when ye come, and all the flowers are dying,
If I am dead, as dead I well may be,
You'll come and find the place where I am lying,
And kneel and say an Ave there for me.
And I shall hear, though soft you tread above me,
And all my grave will warmer, sweeter be,
For you will bend and tell me that you love me,
And I shall sleep in peace until you come to me."♪

Chapter 16. Life, death and humanity

Life is what you make of it, so make it your own. Death is evitable, we've all been forewarned. Humanity speaks volumes without uttering a word, makes you think; are you kind, are you civil, or just downright absurd?

****

"Never regret being a good person to the wrong people. Your behavior says everything about you, and their behavior says enough about them."

***

"Never be ashamed of what you've been through. God will use your story for his GLORY."

***

"One of the best things about getting older: knowing someone is an asshole before they even speak."

***

"You gotta love living baby,
because dying is a pain in the ass." Sinatra

***

"Death, so called, is a thing which makes men weep, and yet a third of life is passed in sleep." Lord Byron

***

"If you don't stand up for what you believe in— you'll fall for anything."

***

"Dream as if you'll live forever, live as if you'll die tomorrow." James Dean

***

"Never discourage anyone who continually makes progress, no matter how slow." Plato

***

"Friends are a blessing, family can be a burden."

***

"Children must be taught now to think, not what to think."

***

"Money is the root—friends become the problem."

***

"Freedom of speech sometimes falls on deaf ears."

***

"It doesn't matter what people call you, it's what you answer to."

***

"Fall in love with healing yourself."

***

"Eat well, live long, laugh much."

***

"Jesus said to go out a build a church, out of ourselves."

***

"God never uses money as a reward, why do Parents."

***

"Many are called, but few are chosen."

***

"How do your children see you as an obstacle or a super-hero?"

***

"You learn nothing from life
if you think you're right all the time."

***

"It's better to live one day as a lion then a hundred as a lamb."
John Gotti

***

"Tell me how I am to breathe with no Heir?" Henry VIII

***

"Never argue with stupid people they will drag you down to their level and then beat you with experience." Mark Twain

***

"A goal without a plan is just a wish."

***

"I'm not brave anymore darling. I'm all broken. They've broken me." Ernest Hemingway

***

"You can always make money—
you can't always make memories."

***

"Never upset an Italian woman.
They remember stuff that hasn't even happened yet!"

***

"The greatest deception men suffer is from their own opinion."
Leonardo Da Vinci

***

"What you tell yourself every day will either lift you up or tear you down."

***

"Life isn't about finding yourself. Life is about creating yourself." George Bernard Shaw

***

"I know what I bring to the table…so trust me when I say I'm not afraid to eat alone."

***

"It's possible to own too much. A man with one watch knows what time it is; a man with two watches is never quite sure."
Lee Segall

***

"I will not let anyone walk through my mind with their dirty feet." Mahatma Gandhi

***

"I walk slowly, but I never walk backwards." Abraham Lincoln

***

"You need to remember, even when you fall flat on your face, you are still moving forward."

***

"During a disaster we evacuate women and children first. So we can think about a solution in silence."

***

"Social Media is training us to compare our lives, instead of appreciating everything we are. No wonder why everyone is always depressed." Bill Murray

***

"Be around those who feed your soul, not eat it."

***

"Never discuss cheese with rats, talk bread with birds
or make moves with snakes."

***

"She leaves a little bit of sparkle wherever she goes."
Kate Spade RIP (suicide 6/2018)

***

"Yankee credo: Make do with what you have."

***

"Mess with the Bull—you get the horns." Easy A

***

"Good fences make good neighbors."

***

"A real man will make: Missing you a hobby, caring for you
his job. Making you happy his duty and loving you his life."

***

"We live in a generation of emotionally weak people.
Everything has to be watered down because it's offensive,
including the truth." Keanu Reeves

***

"Life's blows cannot break a person whose spirit is warmed at
the fire of enthusiasm." Norman Vincent Peale

***

"Live like it's your last day on Earth, love like you just got
married and laugh like you haven't got a trouble in the world."

***

"Live your life and forget your age."

***

"Life is short, break the RULES, FORGIVE quickly, KISS slowly, LOVE truly, LAUGH uncontrollably and NEVER REGRET anything that made you SMILE."

***

"To climb steep hills requires a slow pace at first." Henry VIII

***

"Loyalty & Respect goes both ways. If they don't return it, they don't deserve it."

***

"Trust is more valuable than love, because you can't love someone you don't trust."

***

"If you do not think about the future, you cannot have one."

***

"Life is like a camera. Just focus on what's important. Capture the good times, develop from the negatives and if things don't work out—just take another shot."

***

"Thinking isn't agreeing or disagreeing, that's voting." Robert Frost

***

"In three words I can sum up everything I've learned about life: IT GOES ON." Robert frost

***

"There are few hours in life more agreeable than the hour dedicated to ceremony known as afternoon tea."
Henry James Portrait of a Lady

***

"I put my heart and soul into my work
and have lost my mind in the process." Vincent Van Gogh

***

"Your mind is the garden, your thoughts are the seeds, the harvest can either be flowers or weeds." William Wordsworth

***

"He opened a window in my heart and the light of the world shinned in." David Letterman on the birth of his son

***

"Continuous effort, not strength or intelligence, is the key to unlocking our potential." Sir Winston Churchill

***

"Be a good listener. Your ears will never get you in trouble."
Frank Tyger

***

"It has become my philosophy of life that difficulties vanish when faced boldly." Isaac Asimov

***

"God gave us one tongue and two ears
so we could hear twice as much as we speak"

***

"Nowadays people know the price of everything
and the value of nothing" Oscar Wilde

***

"No one is more hated than he who speaks the truth" Plato

***

"10% of conflicts are due to difference in opinion.
90% are due to wrong tone of voice."

***

"Never give up on something that you can't go a day without
thinking about" Winston Churchill

***

"The 7 deadly sins:
Pride, Envy, Gluttony, Lust, Anger, Greed and Sloth."

***

"The 7 Heavenly virtues:
Faith, Hope, Charity, Fortitude, Justice, Temperance and
Prudence."

***

"I never sleep because sleep is the cousin of death" Somnus in
Roman mythology, death, was his twin.

***

"Respect is earned. Honesty is appreciated. Trust is gained. Loyalty is returned" Tony Soprano

***

"The moon won't use the door only the window" Rumi

***

"If you want to live a happy life tie it to a goal, not to people or objects" Albert Einstein

***

"Not all storms come to disrupt your life; some come to clear your path."

***

"Behind every successful person is a pack of haters."

***

"By the time a child is 4 years old their character is already formed."

***

"Whenever someone did something wrong, Dad always said 'Why would you put smartness in that?'" Louis Lacey

***

"You can't cry on a diamonds shoulder, and diamonds won't keep you warm at night, but they are sure fun when the sun shines." Elizabeth Taylor

***

"You must expect great things of yourself
before you can do them" Michael Jordan

***

"Don't dig-up in doubt what you planted in faith"
Elizabeth Elliot

***

"Don't be afraid: the Queens blood has long rundown into the
earth. And on the spot where it was spilled, grapevines are
growing today." Mikhail Bulgakov

***

"If you're sad add more lipstick and attack."

***

"Sometimes you just need an adventure to cleanse the bitter
taste of life from your soul."

***

"The only time to eat diet food
while waiting for the steak to cook" Julia Child

***

"Perhaps this is the moment for which you have been created"
Esther 4:14

***

"Never let your sense of morals get in the way of doing what's
right" Isaac Asimov

***

"Find something you're passionate about and keep tremendously interested in it." Julia Child

***

"Intelligence without ambition is a bird without wings" Salvador Dali

***

"It's not what happens to you, but how you react to it that matters." Epictetus, Roman Philosopher

***

"Waste of wealth is sometimes returned, waste of health is seldom returned and waste of time is never returned."

***

"If you judge a book by its cover, you'll never know the whole story."

***

"What have you gained if you've forsake yourself?"

***

"Anger is the wind that blows out the light of reason."

***

"Knowing the scripture is one thing, knowing the author is another."

***

"Those who think the world owes them a living, are often too lazy to work themselves."

***

"Failure can be seen as a dead-end
or summons to greater creativity."

***

"Life is a wonderful thing—not things."

***

"To cement relationships listen rather than broadcast."

***

"Anger is only one letter away from DANGER."

***

"Reputation is the other fellow's idea of character."

***

"The best tranquilizer is a clear conscious."

***

"When the church service is over, yours begins."

***

"If criticism could cause one to quit—
the skunk would be extinct."

***

"When we discuss we show our intelligence,
when we argue we show our ignorance."

***

"A child who knows the value of a dollar will ask for two."

***

"Not all wild things can be tamed; maybe they need to find someone as wild as them to roam with."

***

"There is no such thing as a terrible person, just a poor miss-guided soul."

***

"How old are you? I'm as old as my tongue and just as old as my teeth."

***

"The voice of God speaks through tradition."

***

"Do you think it ends because we don't see each other?"

***

"When they're gone where does the love go?"

***

"God doesn't judge people till their dead, why do you?"

***

"No one became very good or very bad suddenly."

***

"Rain falls because the clouds can no longer handle the weight. Tears fall because the heart can no longer handle the pain."

***

"We were all humans until: Race disconnected us,
Religion separated us and politics divided us."

***

"Three things to know in life, never beg anyone. Never trust
anyone and never depend on anyone. Just do it." Evelyn Lacey

***

"None of us are getting out of here Alive. So stop treating
yourself like an after-thought. Eat the delicious food. Walk in
the sunshine. Jump in the ocean. Say the truth that you're
carrying in your heart like a hidden treasure. Be silly. Be kind.
Be weird."

***

"There is no time for anything else" Keanu Reeves

***

"I believe in God. Not because my parents told me to. Not
because a church told me so,
but because I've experienced how awesome he is."

***

"Everything will fall into place;
you just gotta be patient and trust in God."

***

"When my niece Ashley was born she gave me courage, when
she died at 3years of age, that courage got me through."

***

"No matter how many times a snake sheds its skin; it will always be a snake. Remember that before allowing people back into your life."

***

"A special breakfast for your day: a plate of love, a bowl of peace, a spoon of hope, a fork of care and a glass of prayer. Enjoy your meal for you are under God's care."

***

"Why is it so easy to give advice and so hard to take it?"

***

"Sometimes God's greatest gifts are unanswered prayer."

***

"Never frown in public because you will never know who is falling in love with your SMILE" ☺

***

"Don't cry because it's over and done, smile because it happened."

***

"Don't try so hard, the best things happen when you least expect it."

***

"Friends are angels who lift us to our feet when our wings forget how to fly."

***

"A casino is a place where they have what it takes,
to take what you have."

***

"On the road or in an argument when you see RED, stop,"

***

"It's better to make a few new mistakes
than repeat the old ones."

***

"Remember there is no pain and suffering in heaven."

***

"Excellence knows no gender."

***

"In the Fall I'm British. In Winter I'm Victorian. In Spring I'm
French and in Summer I'm as American, as apple pie." me

***

"There is no 'I' in Team, there is one in Vision and I see
myself working alone."

***

"The elevator of life has too many floors make sure you see
them all before getting off at the penthouse."

***

"Live so people want your autographs not your fingerprints."

***

"Life is fragile handle with prayers."

***

"It's not important who was wrong,
but that you admitted I was right."

***

"When you blame your genes, you're really blaming yourself."

***

"You can get people to conform if you LEAD rather than
PUSH."

***

"Pardon is the sweet smell of VICTORY."

***

"If you can't see the forest for the trees, you'll never
understand your children."

***

"The price you pay for fame, don't let it cost you your soul."

***

"In dealing with children do you find yourself in unfamiliar
territory?"

***

"The more you grow-up the less you blow-up."

***

"You can't win respect by demanding it."

***

"When all is said and done will you be remembered for your contributions or your complications?"

***

"Television is the appliance that changes children from irresistible forces to irremovable objects."

***

"There is a fine line between co-worker and friend."

***

"Anyone can be a push-over;
it takes a certain kind of person to push forward."

***

"Don't lose your receipt, maybe you can exchange your attitude?"

***

"Don't bury the pain—experience it."

***

"Are you sorry for what you did,
or are you sorry you got caught?"

***

"If who you know got you this far,
what you know will get you through."

***

"Nostalgia is like a Grammar Lesson—you find the present
tense and the past perfect."

***

"When we die, we leave all that we have
and take all that we are."

***

"Every once in a while
you have to do some mental house cleaning."

***

"Sometimes you have to get mad before the healing begins."

***

"If you're not working towards Peace, War will happen."

***

"People who pray don't worry, people who worry don't pray."

***

"There are 4 stages in dealing with loss, Shock, Denial, Anger
and Acceptance. Some spend their time in anger and never find
acceptance." Rick Springfield

***

"If you died tomorrow did you live today to its fullest?"

***

"You can only push a person so far
before they fall off the cliff."

***

"If you can find humor in life,
you will always see your way through it."

***

"Sometimes the truth hurts."

***

"While on vacation be anyone you like."

***

"Maybe God had a bigger plan than what I had for myself."

***

"The worst thing about growing older,
dealing with your children's advice."

***

"Christ came as bread rather than birthday cake for a reason."

***

"What life is really about, you really can't buy?"

***

"When everything is said and done,
will they remember YOU?"

***

"Dare to be different."

***

"Falling out of love depends on how strong you are."

***

"In school I was the odd ball,
my parents were happily married."

***

"Love is so blind it feels right even when it's wrong."

***

"A man with no goals is like a car with no gas—USELESS."

***

"A bruised limb will heal; a bruised heart just takes longer."

***

"As long as there is breath—there is hope."

***

"Look in his eyes and see the truth."

***

"If I died today, did I do everything I wanted?"

***

"Get back to basics…The BIBLE"

***

"Find it in yourself to be loving,
kind and caring and you will find it in others."

***

"If knowledge is Power, then why do powerful people make unknowledgeable decisions?"

***

"A bank will give you money when you don't need it and refuse you when you do."

***

"If money can't buy happiness, maybe I should lease?"

***

"There is no other feeling so grand than making it on your own."

***

"He who does not understand history is doomed to repeat it."

***

"Take every day like a bag of rice, one grain at a time."

***

"Time may be a great healer, but it's lousy at beautification."

***

"When it's your time to go, it's your time to go."

***

"Time goes by too quickly, only take what you want from it, and let the negative go."

***

"If Chicken soup is Jewish Penicillin
then Chocolate is the cure."

***

"Every person who dies leaves a GOSPEL according to them."
Fr. Mark Dinardo

***

"Magazines are invitations to become educated, entertained
and inspired." me

***

"Make every day PALM SUNDAY, get out there and shake
some hands why don't ya?"

***

"Curiosity killed the surprise."

***

"You can tell how healthy one is by what they take two at a
time, steps or pills."

***

"Old bus drives never die they just transfer."

***

"Life is precious, spend yours wisely."

***

"Food taste better when you share it with someone."

***

"Life is what happens while you are waiting for fame."

***

"Trying to keep my mind right, my soul straight,
and my heart strong."

***

"Those who think there is a TIME LIMIT when GRIEVING...
have never lost a piece of their heart."

***

"An eye for an eye only leads to more blindness."

***

"You must close the door to your past in order to open the
window to your future."

***

"The hardest thing to govern is the heart."

***

"You are something worth waiting for."

***

"Parenting is like a walk in the park—Jurassic Park,"

***

"It's strange that fall is so beautiful, yet everything is dying."

***

"Sometime in your life, you will learn to be your own best
friend."

***

"Attitudes are contagious—make yours worth catching."

***

"Each day I put my head to my pillow and know I'm getting stronger, because I faced another day without you,"

***

"He said 'don't you feel lonely in your own little world' she whispered 'don't you feel powerless living in other peoples world.'"

***

"If you ever wonder what love really is…"

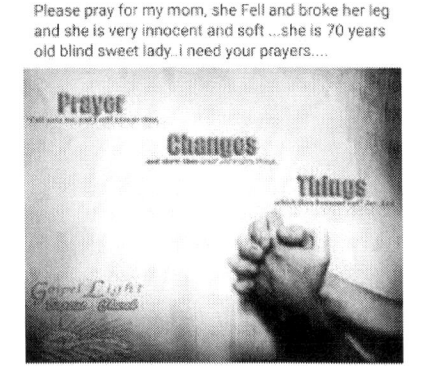

Please pray for my mom, she Fell and broke her leg and she is very innocent and soft …she is 70 years old blind sweet lady..i need your prayers….

Chapter 17. Look to the Rainbow

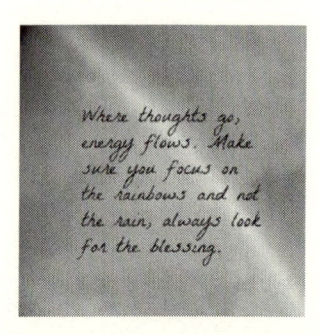

Maybe the Mayans predicted by far. Not an asteroid or a solar flare, but the end of who we are. We no longer cherish life, the living, or earth. We are plagued by war while making our worth. Animal cruelty and greed, a sign of the times, as murder and abuse become splattered headlines. Everyone's preoccupied watching storage wars, while tragedy lingers, just beyond our doors. God's promise to Noah was the all mighty rainbow; full of color and cheer, look around my friends, maybe the end is already near.

****

"Marriages don't break-up because of infidelity
that's just the symptom."

***

"Be stubborn about your goals
and flexible about your methods."

***

"I believe in you—words that water flowers."

***

"When we release anything that's weighing us down,
we can fly higher."

***

"Sobriety is a choice, serenity is a gift."

***

"Life is a beautiful thing, and it's even better when you spend
it with the right people."

***

"Mother Theresa—Nun of the above,"

***

"Difficult roads often lead to beautiful destinations."

***

"Accept what is, let go of what was,
and have faith in what will be."

***

"I don't believe in regrets, I believe your future is in your
tomorrows." John Travolta

***

"The struggle you're in today is developing the strength you
will need for tomorrow."

***

"The best thing I ever did was believe in me."

***

"A bad attitude is like a flat tire, if you don't change it, you'll never go anywhere."

***

"Maybe if we tell people the brain is an APP—
they will start using it."

***

"Everything happens for a reason. We may not understand the wisdom, but we simply have to trust that more will be revealed, and pray to God for continued strength and support."

***

"Quit blaming your parents for everything wrong in your life. Be grateful they saw you through your teenage years and didn't kill you."

***

"Never try to fuck-up someone's life with a lie when yours can be destroyed with the truth."

***

"You can't reach what's in front of you
until you let go of what's behind you."

***

"You've only got three choices in life:
Give up, give in, or give it all you got."

***

"How do you spell Love?
You don't, spell it—you feel it."

***

"As long as God keeps waking you up,
he's not done with you yet."

***

"Logic will get you from A to B.
Imagination will take you everywhere." Albert Einstein.

***

"Some people will only love you as much as they can use you.
Their loyalty ends where the benefits stop."

***

"The Lord will fight for you; you need only be still."

***

"He looked beyond my faults and saw my needs."

***

"There are far better things ahead,
than we leave behind." Rosa Parks

***

"How can I hold my head up high
when I'm not accomplishing anything, anymore?"

***

"Failure is impossible." Susan B. Anthony

***

"I had no idea history was being made,
I was just tired of giving-up." Rosa Parks

***

"I think part of the reason why we hold on to someone so tight is because we fear something so great won't happen twice."

***

"You must never be fearful about what you are doing when it's right." Rosa Parks

***

"Stand for something or you will fall for anything. Today's mighty oak is yesterday's nut that held its ground."

***

"Before you start pointing fingers,
make sure your hands are clean."

***

"A mind is like a parachute, it doesn't work if it isn't open."

***

"Don't get confused between my personality and my attitude.
My personality is who I am;
my attitude depends on who you are."

***

"Be careful who you call your friend; I would rather have 4 quarters than 100 pennies." Susan B. Anthony

***

"Growth is painful. Change is painful. But nothing is as painful as staying stuck somewhere you don't belong."

***

"The loudest BOOS come from the cheap seats."

***

"Growing up means
realizing a lot of your friends aren't really your friends."

***

"If you enjoy it, you understand it."

***

"Your network determines your net worth."

***

"Money isn't everything,
but it ranks right up there with oxygen."

***

"Great ideas often receive
violent opposition from mediocre minds."

***

"One day, the people who didn't believe in you, will tell
everyone they meet, how they know you."

***

"Everyone knows that if you are too careful, you are so
occupied in being careful that you are sure to stumble over
something" Gertrude Stein

***

"My goal is to build a life I don't need a vacation from."

***

"Success doesn't come from what you do occasionally; it comes from what you do constantly."

***

"We repeat what we don't repair."

***

"The road to success is always under construction."

***

"Don't think of cost, think of value."

***

"Being a candle is not easy; in order to give light you must first burn." Rumi

***

"You are what you do, not what you say you do."

***

"The effect you have on others is the most valuable currency there is" Jim Carrey

***

"Try a little harder to be a little better." Gordon B. Hinckley

***

"The better you are at communicating, negotiating and handling your fear of rejection, the easier life is."

***

"How can you feel 6 feet tall when you're barely 5 feet?"
ATTITUDE

***

"Seek Peace and pursue it." Psalms 34:14

***

"There are never enough hours in the day of a Queen,
and her nights have too many."

***

"Elegance is not the prerogative of those who have just escaped
adolescence, but of those who have already taken possession of
the future" Coco Chanel

***

"You'll never find a rainbow
if you're looking down." Charlie Chaplin

***

"Let me be something every minute of every hour of my life."
A tree grows in Brooklyn.

***

"Simplicity is always in Vogue."

***

"Who are you to stand in my way?"

***

"Some people's nerves are so bad
that sleep in church is impossible."

***

"Mind over matter, if you don't mind it don't matter."

***

"The family dinner table is your news station—tune in."

***

"Cause and Effect, you can't have one without the other."

***

"Making a living is not the same thing as making a life."

***

"Money is like Air, you need it to survive."

***

"If you don't enjoy what you're doing,
your paycheck will reflect it."

***

"The higher up the corporate ladder—
the farther you are from reality."

***

"Ask me no question, I tell you no lie."

***

"Freedom of speech sometimes falls into the wrong hands."

***

"Shhh did you hear that? Life is passing you by."

***

"Just build a bridge and get over it."

***

"Mirror, Mirror…what the Fuck Happened?"

***

"Calm, cool and collected, best way to start the day."

***

"All of my treasures fit under one roof."

***

"City people never know their neighbors; country people never know their population."

***

"Marriage is Reality—cheating is fantasy or worse the drug."

***

"Into every life some rain shall fall."

***

"You can make many plans,
but the Lords purpose will prevail."

***

"Dead owls don't give a—HOOT."

***

"A picture is worth a thousand words."

***

"If it's going to be, it's up to me."

***

"The Rainbow—God's promise to Noah,"

***

PAST is experience

PRESENT is experiment

FUTURE is expectation

So better use your experience in your experiment
to meet your expectations.

***

"Art does not exist only to entertain, but also to challenge one
to think, to provoke, even to disturb, in a constant search for
truth." Barbra Streisand

***

"I can take any truth—just don't lie to me."

***

"Don't rain on my parade."

***

Chapter 18. Here and Now

Your LOGO is your smile that brightens any room. Your BUSINESS CARD is your personality that lingers like perfume, and most important is your TRADEMARK, it's like a flower in glorious bloom.

****

"Why doesn't junk mail ever get lost?"

***

"I heard on the whisper."

***

"Life, liberty and getting away with shit,"

***

"Sell the problem you solve, not the product."

***

"Time is the most valuable thing one can spend."

***

"Quality is remembered long after price is forgotten."

***

"Fame comes on and off the stage."

***

"Going out in the world is easy;
making your mark is a test of self."

***

"I want two things from you, Silence and Distance."

***

"Tell me what you ate today and I'll guess who you are."

***

"When SHIT happens, turn into FERTILIZER."

***

"It's hard to kiss your lips at night when you chew my ass-out
all day."

***

"Leaders don't create followers. They create more leaders."

***

"When God created you, he was showing-off."

***

"If he's dumb enough to get caught,
he's dumb enough to be known."

***

"When you are down to nothing, God is up to something."

***

"Hamburger Heaven, what's your beef?"

***

"Thank God for what you have, trust God for what you need."

***

"Hatred is self-punishment."

***

"Children are not only deductible, they are taxing."

***

"Drifting people are like ICEBURGS, wherever they go they
lower the temperature."

***

"If you rock the boat, it may be you that gets sea sick."

***

"Don't change the message, let the message change you."

***

"Clinton was more crooked than a hillbilly smile."

***

"In this country we love to create saints and then tear them down."

***

"Naturally gifted, naturally lifted,"

***

"You can tell how big people are, by what it takes to discourage them."

***

"Some minds are like concrete,
mixed up and permanently set."

***

"There are only two days in the year that nothing can be done. One is called YESTERDAY and the other is called TOMORROW, so TODAY is the right day to love, believe, do and mostly, live."

***

"Life is about making an impact, not making a living."

***

"The afternoon knows what the morning never suspected."
Robert Frost

***

"Home is where your life happens."

***

"If you're not part of the solution, you're part of the problem."

***

"Always be careful of what you hear about a woman. Rumors either come from a man that can't have her, or a woman that can't compete with her."

***

"Deep down you already know the truth."

***

"Your energy introduces you before you even speak."

***

"Almost every successful person begins with two beliefs:
the future can be better than the present.
And I have the power to make it so."

***

"Do what you feel in your heart to be right, for you'll be criticized anyway." Eleanor Roosevelt

***

"If it doesn't challenge you, it won't change you."

***

"Forgiveness: loving yourself enough to move on."

***

"The person, who invented college, never went to college."
Remember that

***

"There are only two choices; make progress or make excuses."

***

"You can either manipulate you circumstances toward success, or you can allow them to dictate your future."

***

"Be so good, they can't ignore you."

***

"Thoughts become dreams, if you see it in your dreams; you will hold it in your hands."

***

"Everything works, not everything works for you."

***

"Creativity takes courage." Matisse

***

"There is a voice that doesn't use words—Listen" Rumi

***

"Eat, sleep, create."

***

"Be as you wish to seem." Socrates

***

"A boss tells you what you can do to achieve a goal. A leader asks what you can do to advance a vision." Simon Sinek

***

"You can't sell your soul for peace of mind."

***

"There's something about a women with a loud mind who sits
in silence, smiling, knowing she can crush you with the truth."
R.G Moon

***

"Be a voice, not an echo."

***

"Don't grieve.
Anything you lose comes around in another form." Rumi

***

"Die with memories, not dreams."

***

"Sell your cleverness and buy bewilderment." Rumi

***

"To be successful your focus has to be so intense that others
think you're crazy."

***

"You can't change your situation;
you can only change how you deal with it."

***

"People don't buy goods and services;
they buy relations, stories and magic." Seth Godin

***

"It's not who you are that holds you back,
it's who you think you're not."

***

"Don't trade your authenticity for approval."

***

"These pains your feel are messages listen to them." Rumi

***

"Everything comes to you at the right time,
be patients with the process."

***

"If you don't see great riches in your imagination,
you will never see it in your bank account."

***

"I don't fear commitment, I fear wasting time."

***

"What we fear doing most,
is usually what we most need to do"
Ralph Waldo Emerson

***

"Speak only if it improves the silence" Gandhi

***

"People who avoid failure also avoid success."

***

"Anxiety happens when you think you have to figure it all out at once, breath, relax and pray."

***

"Bullshit may get you through the door, but brains and know how will keep you there."

***

"Pretend every person you meet has a sign on their head that reads 'make me feel important.'
Not only will you succeed in sales, but in life too."
Mary Kay Ash

***

"If people like you, they will listen to you; if they trust you they'll do business with you."

***

"Be a resource, not a sales pitch."

***

"Don't deliver a product, deliver an experience."

***

"Beach Rules: No shirt, no shoes, bathing suit optional. No skinny dippin alone. No drinking till 5pm somewhere."

***

"Be helpful. When you see a person without a smile, give them yours."

***

"You are not a drop in the ocean;
you are the entire ocean in one drop." Rumi

***

"Wisdom is knowing what to do, Skill is knowing how to do it,
and Virtue is doing it well."

***

"Tell people what they want to hear,
and you can sell them anything."

***

"Confidence is like a muscle;
the more you use it the strong it gets."

***

"When you want something bad enough,
all the universe conspires in helping you to achieve it."

***

"Don't give up, if you do, the next person in line is ready to
take it away from you."

***

"Don't let the fear of striking out
keep you from playing the game."

***

"If you get tired learn to rest, not quit."

***

"It's hard to stop someone who never quits." James Bond

***

"Things to know about life, 'No.' is a complete sentence. It does not require justification or explanation."

***

"If you don't love yourself, you'll always be chasing after people who don't love you either." Mandy Hale

***

"We cannot solve our problems with the same thinking we used when we created them." Albert Einstein

***

"Never confuse movement with action." Ernest Hemingway

***

"A healthy attitude is contagious, but don't wait to catch it from others. Be a carrier." Tom Stoppard

***

"The goal of criticism is to leave people with the feeling they've been helped."

***

"When the door is shut, tis better to knock."

***

"Why am I unhappy with everything I want?"

***

"The best way to get over a bad relationship is to move forward in the opposite direction."

***

"There isn't enough room in your mind for both WORRY and Faith. You must decide which one will live there."

***

"What do you call a happy person on a Monday—RETIRED"

***

"Your parents created a miracle; don't let society turn you into a time-bomb."

***

"Spring has sprung, the orange barrels are back."

***

"If you're breathing, it's never too late."

***

"Money is at your fingertips, spending, earning and saving."

***

"Religion is the Opium of the Masses."

***

"Get back to basics; it's all about knowing when you've gone too far."

***

"People take examples far more seriously than advice."

***

"Don't pretend to be what you don't intend to be."

***

"It's what we are that gets across, not what we teach."

***

"Those who don't fear God fear everything else."

***

"Believe in what you do."

***

"Honor sometimes fades when one enters Politics."

***

"Confidence is the feeling you have before you know better."

***

"A school is only as good as its teachers."

***

"There is always room for dessert."

***

"If you're not a people person, you'll always be alone."

***

"STRESSED spelled backwards is DESSERTS,
so have some UPSIDE DOWN cake."

***

"The elderly struggle to buy food or Medication, is this the American way?"

***

"TIME decides who you meet in your life."

***

"Only a dumb person thinks money makes you smart."

***

"Hatred is a product of environment; it's not in the genes."

***

"Your HEART decides who you want in your life."

***

"In the land of thieves what happens when one says NO?"

***

"The 'Golden Rule' is beginning to tarnish."

***

"Your BEHAVIOUR decides who will stay in your life."

***

"Make today so awesome yesterday gets jealous."

***

"My other car is a YACHT."

***

"I wish people would be as obsessed with God as they are in finding ELVIS."

***

"We either make ourselves miserable or we make ourselves strong, the amount of work is the same."

***

"Complaining about a problem without a solution—
is called whining."

***

"These mountains that you are carrying,
you were only supposed to climb."

***

"People will forget your harsh words, they will even forget what you did, but they will never forget the way you treated them."

***

"You see in the world—what you have in your heart."

***

"Not in your time—but in His time."

***

Chapter 19. God Answers knee Mail

God's been answering knee mail through all of the ages, so clear and refine as if written on pages. Silent prayers go up, as blessings come down, confirming our faith is all around. Most of us pray with so much to say, but please remember—there's no right or wrong way.

****

The 12 fruits of the holy spirit, Charity, joy, peace, patience, kindness, goodness, generosity, gentleness, faithfulness, modesty, self-control and chastity…Galatians 5:22-23

***

"A.S.A.P: **A**lways **S**ay **A** **P**rayer."

***

"The 7 gifts of the Holy Spirit: Wisdom, understanding, counsel, fortitude, knowledge, piety, and fear of the Lord."

***

"No Hater can stop God's favor. God will give them front row seats to watch him bless you."

***

"Pick up the bible it will feed you more than takeout."

***

"Angel of God, my guardian dear, to whom God's love commits me here, ever this day be at my side, to light and guard, to rule and guide."

***

"Anxiety is another version of atheism,"

***

"God doesn't waste miracles."

***

"The more I go to church and the more I turn myself over to the process of believing in Jesus and listening to His Word and having Him guide my hand. I feel as though the pressure is off me now." Sylvester Stallone

***

"God hears a mother's prayer." Victoria Gotti

***

"The Church is like a great ship being pounded by the waves of life's different stresses. Our duty is not to abandon ship, but to keep her on her course." St. Boniface

***

"Pray so big and so often that when God meets you at Heaven's Gate, he says with a smile 'Kid, you kept me very busy.' "

***

"The only way is the holy way."

***

"I was raised Catholic, so every time I hear 'May the force be with you' my natural response is 'and with your spirit.'"

***

"God will never let you down, God will never leave. God will never hurt you. God will never lie. God will never cheat. God is always faithful."

***

"God is the biggest help in the world."

***

"Comparisons destroy relationships." Fr. Mark

***

"Holy Mary—shortest way to Christ."

***

"Be the light that God see's in you."

***

"Watch-out success is always an option."

***

"The ways and means are always front and center."

***

"This man was expelled from 14 schools, dropped out of college to pursue acting. Went on 1000s of auditions and still couldn't get work. Evicted from his apartment, he slept in a bus station for weeks. So desperate for money he took roles in porn movies. With $100 to his name he finally got his big break at 30 years old—Sylvester Stallone"

***

"Read the bible to be wise, believe the bible to be safe and practice the bible to be holy."

***

"If you have to tell someone you're Catholic, you already messed-up."

***

"When counting my blessings I count you twice."

***

"A catholic life is a pilgrimage not a sight-seeing tour."

***

"Penance restores peace of mind and heart."

***

"Jesus is the way, he will never mislead you."

***

"Going to church will not make you a Catholic any more than going into a garage will make you a mechanic."

***

"People are always pretending they are smarter than they are."

***

"Love one another as I have loved you." God

***

"You can't PRAY to God on Sunday and prey on your friends
the rest of the week."

***

"When a door closes somewhere God opens a window."

***

"Give God a laugh, tell him your plan."

***

"When our head is cluttered,
prayers help organize our thoughts."

***

"God brings the good into your life—if you let him."

***

"Show and Tell, God wants you to."

***

"If you want to know what God thinks of money,
just look at who has it."

***

"When GOD looks down upon me, do I make him proud?"

***

"God's presence is not a limited engagement."

***

"If today you hear Gods Voice, harden not your heart."

***

"It's not easy being Catholic;
you have to work at it every day."

***

"Substance abuse is no cure for Spiritual Problems."

***

"God doesn't make deals he sends blessings,
the secret is to find them in everyday life."

***

"God does not care how much money you make—
it's what you do with it that Matters."

***

"Anytime, Anyplace, Anywhere…God is there."

***

"The Bible—it's all there in black and white."

***

"Life on earth is boot-camp,
for our eternity in heaven." Fr. Mark Dinardo

***

"Should I be greedy and please myself or should I share and please God?"

***

"Confession cleans the soul."

***

"God is all around; you must look with your heart, not your eyes."

***

"If you lived in the time of Jesus, would you follow or condemn?"

***

"Faith is what helps us deal with reality."

***

"Keep the faith. The most amazing things happen in life tend to happen right at the moment you're about to give up hope."

***

"When GOD pushes you to the edge of difficulty—trust him fully, because two things will happen, either he will catch you when you fall, or he will teach you how to fly."

***

"As prayers go up, blessings go come down."

***

"The Closer you get to your blessing the harder the devil will try to attack your mind, body, soul and spirit, stay focused."

***

"Jesus hears your tears like a prayer."

***

"Jewish people believe God counts the tears of woman."

***

"Don't let anyone take you back
to what God brought you through."

***

"God provides strength for the tasks and trials of life."

***

"Prayer is the key to heaven, but Faith unlocks the door."

***

"When life seems difficult, P.U.S.H…
Pray Until Something Happens."

***

"Folks ask me if I'm a practicing catholic. I tell them, 'Yes, I
am going to keep practicing until I get it right.'"

***

"Dance like no one is watching."

***

"Just know this is not all there is."

***

"GRACE is when God gives us good things we don't deserve

MERCY is when God spares us from the bad things we deserve.

BLESSINGS are when God is generous with both."

***

"When life gives you more than you can stand, kneel."

***

"The first ever cordless phone was invented by god its called 'prayer' it never loses it signal and you never have to recharge it, use it anywhere."

***

"Life begins at the end of your comfort zone."

***

"They did not leave your life—I moved them…God"

***

The Lord bless you and keep you;
The Lord make His face to shine upon you
To shine upon you and be gracious
And be gracious unto you
The Lord bless you and keep you
The Lord lift up the light of His countenance upon you
The Lord lift up the light of His countenance upon you
And give you peace, and give you peace;

Chapter 20. Girl Talk

Girls talk and chatter is our familiar tone, we laugh, we smart—wherever we roam. Ladies are like brandy, so deep and refine—smiling unknowingly all of the time. Women are forceful, beware of their stare, you have no idea, just how much we can bear. Girls become ladies and ladies become women, it's all about life and how we see them. We've shed our tears throughout the years. We've faced it all and found our voice—strong and mighty was our only choice. sylvia

"She doesn't plan, she plots."

***

"I know I'm a handful, but that's why you have two hands."

***

"If another woman steals your man, there is no better revenge than letting her keep him. Real men can't be stolen."

***

"What I'm looking for, you ain't got"

***

"What was cute at 25…is just stupid at 35."

***

"I want you out of my subconscious—I sub-let-it."

***

"You're not too smart are you—I like that in a man."

***

"I'm more likely to talk to you if I can get a word in."

***

"Shopping is a matter of life and debt."

***

"Stop feeling sorry for your friends."

***

"Do you exercise?—I run my mouth a lot."

***

"The sun does not rise and set on your ass."

***

"A friend indeed in always a friend in need,"

***

"A smile is the best makeup any girl can wear."

***

"Why buy the whole pig
when all you really wanted was a little bit of sausage."

***

"Want me to walk you to your car—
this city ain't safe for a little bitch."

***

"I walked away because you were busy finding faults in me,
while I was busy overlooking you."

***

"Move on gorgeous; there are guys who would beg for your
pretty little heart."

***

"A man who knows of your sadness and sleeps—
doesn't deserve your love at all."

***

"He may wear the pants in the family,
but I tell him which ones to put on."

***

"Be the kind of woman that when your feet hit the floor each
morning the devil says 'Oh crap, she's up!'"

***

"If you don't matter to men of power, you don't matter."

***

"I want to live my life, not record it." Jackie Kennedy

***

"It is hard to be a woman. You must think like a man, act like a lady, look like a young woman and work like a horse."

***

"A good man you might find. A better man will find you.
The best man is who God gives you."

***

"Why can't mosquitoes suck out the fat instead of the blood?"

***

"How old am I—if I was a bottle of wine, you couldn't afford me and if I was a bottle of whiskey, you couldn't handle me!"

***

"Let's remember that our TONGUE holds blessings and curses, so let's watch our words."

***

"There's a good chance that some people don't like me—however there's an even better chance that I don't care."

***

"Wait for the boy that would do anything—
to be your everything,"

***

"Every guy thinks that every girls dream is to find the perfect guy…Please. Every girls dream is to eat without getting fat."

***

"Current relationship status: Made dinner for two, ate both."

***

"Half the fun of doing anything is the outfit you get to wear."

***

"It's not easy being a Princess."

***

"Date the person who tells you to be safe when you go out, not the one who gets mad." Partnership not Ownership

***

"I'm the girl who would eat Doritos on her wedding day and accidentally wipe her hands down her dress."

***

"You don't let go of a bad relationship, because you stop caring about them.
You let go, because you start caring about yourself."

***

"Girls, who don't ask for much, deserve it all."

***

"Just remember all that shit someone puts you through, sooner or later finds its way back to them."

***

"Don't leave what you have at home to go chase what's in the streets. You will regret it."

***

"Some guys just can't handle the responsibility and privilege of having one faithful girl. They want a million hoes."

***

"Above all else conduct yourself with class."

***

"One must not let oneself be overwhelmed by sadness."
Jackie Kennedy

***

"Give me your tired, your poor, your huddled masses yearning to breathe free, the wretched refusal of your teeming shore. Send these, the homeless, tempted-tossed to me; I lift my lamp beside the golden door!" These words appear on a bronze plaque at the base of the Statue of Liberty, thank you Emma Lazarus.

***

"Revenge is beneath me, but accidents happen." Liz Taylor

***

"He made me happy once and it fucked me up for life."

***

"I'm not the appearance, it's the essences, it's not the money, it's the education, it's not the clothes, it's the CLASS."
Coco Chanel

***

"I don't understand how a woman can leave the house without fixing herself up a little if only out of politeness. And then you never know, maybe that's the day she has with destiny. And it's best to be pretty as possible for destiny." Coco Chanel

***

"Elegance is when the inside is as beautiful as the outside."
Coco Chanel

***

"You can't hurt someone who doesn't love you."

***

"You need to learn how to select your thoughts just the same way you select your clothes every day. This is a power you can cultivate." Elizabeth Gilbert 'Eat, Pray, Love'

***

"I may have cut him out of my life, but he's still in my heart."

***

"Finally men who understand women, BEN & JERRY"s"

***

"You can be Gorgeous at thirty, Charming at forty, and IRRESTIBLE for the rest of your life." Coco Chanel

***

"I don't need a man to solve my problems—I need a man who won't be the problem."

***

"A woman with good shoes is never ugly." Coco Chanel

***

"If you want me in your life put me there,
I shouldn't have to fight for a spot."

***

"The best presents come in small packages."

***

"From now on it's all about ME, ME, ME, ME,"

***

"I can tell you're lying, you lips are moving."

***

"If you can't find Mr. Right how about Mr. Right Now?"

***

"When it comes to chocolate, its every girl for herself,"

***

"Men are like onions, each layer reveals who he is."

***

"Never be the number 2 girl, you'll always be shit-on."

***

"Your car is not the only one with a blind spot."

***

"She got the best of you; I got the rest of you."

***

"A man in never the answer, he's just a bigger question."

***

"I want a guy who treats me like nothing but milk—spoils me."

***

"A man can be your knight in shining armor
or the thief in the night."

***

"If she's hot and still single—she's crazy."

***

"Once I get what I want I don't want it anymore."

***

"Why did love walk into my life and then Ran Out?"

***

"First you marry for love; secondly you marry for money,
third time you marry for companionship."

***

"A man who takes and takes, will never give you a happy life."

***

"Face it, I've got needs, and I've got wants,
and I don't need or want you."

***

"Men want a lady in the streets and freak in the sheets."

***

"Never make my business your pleasure."

***

"Never let a man know how much control he has."

***

"Always keep them guessing."

***

"The man I fell for, doesn't exit."

***

"I know how the lady in the Harbor feels…"

***

"My life is passing before my eyes and you ain't in it!"

***

"Beware of woman who dream in chocolate"

***

"Be careful of woman who will love you for who you are, they will settle for anything."

***

"If you let him hurt you—HE WILL."

***

"When it comes to your wedding ring, anything less than 5 carats is an appetizer."

***

"Whatever happened to tall, dark and handsome?"

***

"If he's worth your time, he'll make time for you."

***

"If you love him set him free, if he comes back,
it's meant to be."

***

"Seek and she shall fine—it on sale."

***

"You know what's sexier than a bad boy?
A grown-ass-man with his shit together,"

***

"Whether over coffee, over drinks or over the phone, there is
Girl talk, a quant essential need."

***

"When you have a QUEEN don't reshuffle the deck to end up
with a JOKER."

***

"Marriage is like a deck of cards. In the beginning all you need
is two Hearts and a Diamond. By the end, you wish you had a
CLUB and a SPADE."

***

"If he makes you cry now, he'll make you want to die later,"

***

"My ex was from the land down under, Australia—no HELL."

***

"Do you ever wish you had a second chance to meet someone again for the first time, so you could run the other way?"

***

"Dress like Coco. Live like Jackie. Act like Audrey. Laugh like Lucy."

***

"If I throw a stick, would you leave?"

***

"Love is a four letter word."

***

"Choose your words carefully, once they are said you own them."

***

"She wasn't looking for a knight;
she was looking for a sword." Attious

***

"A coffee a day keeps the grumpy away."

***

"A wise girl knows her limits.
A smart girl knows she has none."

***

"You will never influence the world by trying to be like it."

***

"Be the girl that makes you happy."

***

"The best color in the world—
is the one that looks good on you." Coco Chanel

***

"Men who say women belong in the kitchen, obviously don't
know what to do with them in the bedroom."

***

"The West—Oh honey I'm the Wicked Witch of everything."

***

She is beauty:

Aries, Sagittarius, Virgo Gemini

She is Grace:

Capricorn, Cancer, Pisces, Aquarius

She will punch you in your face:

Scorpio, Leo, Taurus, Libra

Chapter 21. Boys will be Boys

Boys will be boys at any old age; they're daring and peculiar like words on a page. Fables have warned us to guard our dear hearts, yes some are like Marc Anthony, but some are like Bonaparte. Mighty and eccentric they show up on the scene, they want what they want, you know what I mean. But men are a different bread, they're loyal, tried and true, they're chase you, and adore you—ah, what ya gonna do.

****

"Men stopped treating women like ladies
when they started behaving like men."

***

"If you married me, you'd be Mrs. Wonderful."

***

"Being male is a matter of birth. Being a man is a matter of age, but being a gentleman is a matter of choice." Vin Diesel

***

"Her perfume reminds me of freshly picked flowers that permeate the air mixed with a gentle hint of debauchery."

***

"The nicer you treat her outside the bedroom; the naughtier it will get inside the bedroom."

***

"Some people will never like me—and I will never give a fuck!"

***

"It's a man's job to respect a woman,
but it's a woman's job to give him something to respect."

***

"There's a difference between a boy who kinda likes you and a man who needs your soul next to his. Learn the difference."

***

"Classy is when you have a lot to say, but you choose to remain silent in front of fools." George Clooney

***

"Falling in love is easy. Having sex is easier. But bumping into someone that can spark your soul—
that is what life is all about."

***

"You can fuck your whole life up loving the wrong person"

***

"Dress like James Bond. Speak like Hemmingway. Work like Ralph Lauren and Party like Gatsby."

***

"The superior man thinks only of virtue,
the common man thinks only of comfort."

***

"A man, who has committed a mistake and does not correct it,
is committing another one." Confucius

***

"My fellow men of the world: There comes a time in every
man's life when he has to put the video games down. Man-up,
suit-up, and wine & dine the fuck out of a beautiful girl."

***

"Do you believe in love at first sight, or shall I walk by again?"

***

"I've got a long list of Ex-lovers, they'll tell you I'm insane,
but I've got a blank space, baby and I'll write your name."
Henry VIII

***

"Fella's, don't let a $7.00 dollar sundress cost you $70,000
dollars in child support this summer." Erika Heinz

***

"If her bra matches her panties when you take her clothes off,
it wasn't you who decided to have sex."

***

"She is too beautiful. My beer is too cold, and I don't like
bacon—said no guy ever."

***

"Men are born between a woman's legs and spend the rest of their lives trying to get back between them…why—because there is no place like HOME."

***

"True or False? Women ignore nice guys, chase assholes and then complain about it!"

***

"My friend thinks he's smart, he said onions are the only food that makes you cry, so I threw a coconut at his face."

***

"A man's ego is just as fragile as a woman's heart"

***

"If I was a plastic surgeon…
I would put a squeaky toy in every breast implant."

***

"There are only three things that women need in life, food, water and compliments." Chris Rock

***

"Women need a reason to have sex; men just need a place."
Billy Crystal

***

"A man with dreams needs a woman with vision."

***

"Trust me you can dance…Vodka"

***

"Never delay kissing a pretty girl, or opening a bottle of
whiskey," Ernest Hemingway

***

"Men who cater to woman—
will never need or want for anything."

***

"Men are always looking for a B.L.T.
Brains, Looks and Talent"

***

"Most men like their beer COLD and their women HOT."

***

"Wives are like Grenades, remove the ring and Boom, house is
gone."

***

"Know what's on the MENU…Me-N-U."

***

"YOU want to know what the best thing in my life is;
it's the first word of this sentence."

***

"I'll be Burger King, and you be McDonalds.
I'll have it my way, and you'll be lovin it."

***

Chapter 22. Amor, Romance and Tujour

Amor is the reason we laugh, giggle and frown, romance by any means, has its ups and its downs. *Tujours* in French means; to love forever, I couldn't agree more, *mon amour*—the French are so clever.

"Why do we close our eyes when we pray, when we cry, when we kiss or when we dream? Because the most beautiful things in life are not seen, but felt by your heart."

"Sometimes, the people who are thousands of miles away from you, can make you feel better than people right beside you."
me

"Never love anybody who treats you like you're ordinary."
Oscar Wilde"

"Woman fall in love by what hear, men fall in love by what they see, that's why women wear makeup and men lie."
Idris Elba

"When somebody loves you, you feel it in your heart."

"I guess cupid was in disguise, the day you walked in and changed my life. I think it's amazing how love can set you free." George Michael

"Five ways to say sweet in French: Mon amour-my love. Ma Beaute-my beauty. Ma louloute-my honey-pie. Monchaton-my kitten. Mon ange-my angel."

"Love you till the day after forever."

"Promise her anything, but give her love." Dean Martin

"How do you find a lady—start by being a gentleman."

"Love is patience, love is blind,
and love is slowly losing your mind."

"Be the type of man you'd want your daughter to be with."

"You've got the lips that wet my whistle."

"A man's biggest mistake is giving another man the opportunity to make his woman smile."

"With his blessings from above, serve it generously with love. One man, one wife, one love, through life," Dean Martin

"You are not only my greatest pleasure—you are my greatest reward! You are mine." S.K.

"Call it old fashioned, but to respect a woman you love, should be a priority."

"True love is always fueled by lust."

"What each kiss means: a kiss on the forehead—your mine. A kiss on the cheek—we're friends. A kiss on the hand—I adore you. A kiss on the neck—I want you, now. A kiss on the shoulder—you're perfect. A kiss on the lips—I LOVE YOU."

"There is never a bad time to be held and hugged."

"No one has ever written a romance better than we lived it."
Lauren Bacall on Bogart

"A friend for life or a lover for less,"

"What's wrong with you—nothing you can't fix."
Boggie to Bacall

"A true relationship is having someone who accepts your past,
supports your present and encourages your future."

"One of the reasons why I love you—
you make me smile for no reason,"

"That first wedding look, love without words."

"Hold me when I'm sad, kiss me when I cry. Make me laugh
when I'm down and love me till I die."

♫"Return to me, for my heart wants you only. Hurry home,
hurry home, won't you please hurry home to my heart."♪
Dean Martin

"I don't want anyone else to have your heart, kiss your lips, or be in your arms, because that's only my place."

"Happy wife—happy life,"

"Brew me a cup for a winter's night, for the wind howls and furies frights. Spice it with love and stir it with care, and I'll toast your bright eyes my sweetest fair." Sandeep Kumar

"Two souls, but with a single thought, two hearts that beat as one," John Keats

"Fill your paper with the breathings of your heart." William Wordsworth

"I am my beloveds and my beloved is mine." William Wordsworth

"Touch has a memory" John Keats

"My love is selfish—I cannot breathe without you." John Keats

"We were together, I forgot the rest." Walt Whitman

"Get married when you're really ready. Retire with loads of memories. Become an influencer. Fall in love with inner beauty. Make your parents proud of how happy you are. Make real friends. Find happiness in the ordinary. Find someone who you can't live without."

"Love will find a way through paths where wolves fear to prey." Lord Byron

"Friendship may, and often does, grow into love, but love never subsides into friendship." Lord Bryon

"You wanna know who I'm in love with—read the first word."

"Distance isn't an issue the bottom line is—I have you,"

"There is only one happiness in life, to love and be loved."

"You stole my heart but I'll let you keep it."

"Thinking of you keeps me awake; dreaming of you keeps me asleep, being with you keeps alive."

***The Royal Wedding ***

May nineteenth two-thousand and eighteen

Prince Harry married Meghan Markle

"When did I know she was 'The One' the very first time we met," Prince Harry on Megan

"This beautiful woman just literally tripped and fell into my life," Prince Harry

"We are two people who are really happy and in love." Meghan Markle

"I could barely let (him) finish proposing, like 'can I say yes now!?'" Meghan Markle

"I know that at the end of the day she chose me. I chose her. Whatever we have to tackle will be us together as a team." Prince Harry

Congratulations Harry and Meghan

"Love should feel secure, but wild."

"It was not my lips you kissed, but my soul" Judy Garland

"Veni, Vidi, Amavi…we came, we saw, we loved."

"When I'm with you my whole world stands still…
you're my one and only thrill"

"Heaven is where ever you are."

"'Show me your scars,' he said. 'But why?' she asked
quizzically. 'I want to see how many times you needed me and
I wasn't there.'"

"America is my country; Paris is my home town" Gertrude
Stein

"If you really love me, give me wings." Justin Kiriakis

"Love me or leave me or just let me go."

"The average woman falls in love 7 times in her life,
6 are with shoes" Kenneth Cole

"That's why birds do it, bees do it, even educated flees do it,
let's do it, let's fall in love." Cole Porter

"It's always better to marry someone who loves you more than
you love them."

"You keep me safe, I'll keep you wild."

"You do something to me,
something that simply mystifies me" Cole Porter

"A boy will monopolize your time;
a man will capture your heart."

"Olive me loves Olive you & I love you to-ma-toes."

***

"Your lips are like wine and I want to get drunk."

"Make him addicted to you."

"'Where should I apply perfume?' a young girl asked?
'Wherever you want to be kissed' she replied."

"When I'm with you I can look down at the sky."

"Night and day you are the one, only you beneath the moon
and under the sun." Cole Porter

"I have you so deep in my heart, you are part of me."

"After you, who could supply my sky with blue?"

"They say love is the best investment, the more you give, the
more you get." Audrey Hepburn

"I'd rather have bad times with you, than without you."

"I see forever in your eyes."

"Life is not about the amount of breath you take, but who
takes your breath away."

"There is nothing like love in the afternoon."

"Life is love."

"If I had to choose between breathing and loving you I would use my last breath and utter… I love you"

"Love is the thing,"

"Miles separate our hands, but nothing on earth can separate our hearts" Sandeep Kumar

"I love you not because of who you are, but because of who I am when I'm with you."

"No man or woman is worth your tears, and the one who is, won't make you cry."

"Find a guy who smears your lipstick, not your mascara."

"You gave me today; I'll give you tomorrow."

"Follow your heart and you'll find Joy, follow your head and you'll never know."

"A lot of men will come in and out of your life, but very few will dazzle you."

"Your folks must be thieves; they stole a sparkle from the sky and put it in your eye."

"Love is like the wind, I can't see it, but it's there."

"To love another person is to see the face of GOD."

"You must first find yourself before you find someone else."

"He made my pleasure his business."

"God gave you the other half of my heart, we belong together."

"A smile says hello without uttering a word."

"I skinned my knee when I fell for you."

"When you stole 3rd base you stole my heart."
dedicated to Kenny Lofton

"Spread hope instead of despair."

"Alienation of affection equals divorce."

"Love is blind, but friendships are clairvoyant."

"When you love someone make it forever."

"Secret to a long marriage—he always gets his way
and I'm always right."

"There's no such thing as the next best thing to love."

"One day, someone will walk into your life and make you see
why it never worked out with anyone else."

"Amor, amor, amor…"

"They asked him 'How's your life?'

He smiled and answered

'She is fine.' " Sandeep Kumar

"A great relationship is about two things, first, appreciate the similarities and second, respect the differences."

"Love makes things happen."

"Love makes the world go round"

"With you by my side I can do anything."

"For something so intoxicating and addictive she left the most amazing hangover."

"Her lips taste of vodka and jazz –on a rainy afternoon."

"When a man loves a woman, she becomes his weakness. When a woman loves a man, he becomes her strength. This is called an exchange of power."

"He calls me beautiful like it's my name."

"I hadn't any idea an angel could change my life."
Sandeep Kumar

"To the world you may be just a person, but to me, you are more than the world." Sandeep Kumar

"It doesn't matter whether we always agree or disagree. What matters is that I love you and you love me." Sandeep Kumar

"Marriage ends when the fairytale fades"

"To find a man who loves you with all that he has is proof that it's heaven sent."

"Caught up in the rapture of love…"

"Love doesn't need to be perfect; it just needs to be pure."

"It is every woman's dram to be some man's dream woman."

♥♥♥

"Goodbye, no use leading with our chins
this is where our story ends.
Never lovers, ever friends
Goodbye, let our hearts call it a day.

But before you walk away
I sincerely want to say
I wish you bluebirds in the spring
to give your heart a song to sing.

And then a kiss.
But more than this
I wish you love"

Natalie Cole RIP 12/31/2015

Chapter 23. Heartache

Heartache by definition: emotional anguish or grief, typically caused by the loss or absence of someone loved.

Emotional anguish is hard to explain; it rattles and wears heavy on the brain. Grief is something too hard to describe, but we all know the feeling deep down inside. Loss is something we all have to bear; I just hope your love ones will always be there. Absence is that feeling when someone is gone; you're empty and wondering, just what went wrong. Love ones who leave us heartbroken and torn, know the state of our heart, shattered and worn.

****

"One day mom and I were talking and I posed the question 'What would you do if I died before you.' Ma was quiet, so I proceeded. 'Mark is out in Vegas, it's just too damn hot. Tom's house is too small how would you manage and let's not forget Alex, he doesn't have a bathroom on the first floor.' Ma spoke quickly and said 'I'll just go with you.' My mom always took the lighter side of heartache."

****

"I forgive people by forgetting them."

***

"Love can't grow without trust,"

***

"There's no comfort in the truth—pain is all you'll find."
George Michael RIP12/25/2016

***

"Memories often hurt, but sometimes they give hope,"

***

"A light heart will carry you through the hard times."

***

"Please be stronger than your past. The future may still give
you a chance." George Michael

***

"If I feel for you that's my fault—if you abuse that's your sin."

***

"Keep some room in your heart for the unimaginable."

***

"The strongest drug that exists for a human
is another human being."

***

"Only time will set you free."

***

"You get what you settle for."

***

"The lowest depth of misery is betrayal."

***

"Sometimes you can get so busy trying to be everyone else's anchor that you don't even realize you are actually drowning."

***

"Being satisfied is the death of success."

***

"It eventually gets better, without any sort of explanation, you just wake up one morning and you're not as upset anymore."

***

"Why are you trying to fit in when you were born to stand out."

***

"What you fear the most will surely come upon you."

***

"What hurts the most is what we hold onto so tight."

***

"When you fail at planning, you plan to fail."

***

"Why do I love the wrong man—
because the right one never came along."

***

"If it smells like trouble, looks like trouble,
it's probably trouble."

***

"It's important to move on, not run away."

***

"Dare to be the Willow, when the wind blows—
bend instead of break."

***

"People take examples more serious than advice."

***

"Sometimes we don't see it until we're ready to see it."

***

"That chip on your shoulder is the biggest load of all."

***

"Christianity helps us face the music
when we don't like the tune."

***

"If my life were a painting it would be a watercolor."

***

"One day her heart will stop mentioning you."

***

"But he, that dares not grasp the thorn should never crave the rose," Anne Brontë

***

"Gone yet not for gotten although we are apart, your spirit lives within me, forever in my heart,"

***

"I'm not heartless; I just learned how to use my heart less."

***

"The soul usually knows what to do to heal itself. The challenge is to silence the mind."

***

"I just have this happy personality and a sad soul in one body. It feels weird sometimes."

***

"Everyone must choose one of two pains; the pain of discipline or the pain of regret."

***

"Was it hard? I ask 'Letting go?' I nodded 'Not as hard as holding on to something that wasn't real.'"

***

"I am learning to love the sound of my feet walking away from things not meant for me."

***

"When you start seeing your worth, you will find it harder to stay around people who don't."

***

"Sometimes we fall down because there is something down there we're supposed to find."

***

"The reason you can't fix yourself is because you didn't make yourself. God of all creation made you; he knows how to fix you."

***

"Your hardest times often lead to the greatest moments of your life. Keep the faith. It will all be worth it in the end."

***

"If you always do what you always did, you will always get what you always got." Albert Einstein

***

"I don't need any distractions in my life right now. So if you aren't in my life to build with me and grow with me, you're pointless. I'm getting too old for pointless situations, friendships and relationships."

***

"What's meant to be will always find a way."

***

"DEPRESSION—is a flaw in chemistry, not character."

***

"When it's over leave, don't continue watering a dead flower."

***

"Until you start believing in yourself,
you ain't gonna have a life." Rocky

***

"Everyone must choose one of two pains: the pain of discipline
or the pain of regret."

***

"Holding onto anger is like drinking poison and expecting the
other person to die." Buddha

***

"Sometimes the love of your life
comes after the mistake of your life."

***

"First sign of stupidity is inheriting other people's enemies
as a sign of loyalty."

***

"The people in your life should be a source of reducing stress,
not causing more of it."

***

"Inner peace begins the moment you choose not to allow
another person or event to control your emotions."

***

"Stop looking for happiness in the same place you lost it."

***

"It's sad, but sometimes, moving on with the rest of your life starts with—GOODBYE."

***

"Don't be afraid of losing people. Be afraid of losing yourself by trying to please everyone around you."

***

"Faith is seeing light with your heart when all your eyes see is darkness." Ramona Robinson, submitted by Terrie Walls

***

"You were a dream. Then a reality. Now a memory."
Lian Thomas

***

"Isn't it funny how day by day nothing changes, but when you look back, **everything is different**?" C.S. Lewis

***

"If you want it bad enough—stop at nothing."

***

"Living unloved, to die unknown, Unwept, untended and alone." Christina Rossetti

***

"I think it's important to realize that no matter how good you are to people—it won't make them good to you."

***

"Never break four things in your life—trust, promise, relations and heart because when they break they don't make noise, they just pain you a lot."

***

"It's not the years in your life—but the life in your years that counts." Romona Robinson submitted by Terrie Walls

***

"It doesn't matter who hurt you, or broke you down. What matters is who made you smile again."

***

"When you are going through something hard and wonder where God is, remember the teacher is always quiet during the test."

***

"May the constant love of caring friends soften your sadness. May cherished memories bring you moments of comfort. May lasting peace surround your grieving heart."

***

"No matter what your problem is don't nurse it. Don't curse it. Don't rehearse it. Just give it to God and he will reverse it."

***

"Ships don't sink because of the water around them; ships sink because of the water that gets in them. Don't let what's happening around you get inside you and weigh you down."

***

"I'm a slave to my emotions, to my likes, to my hatred of boredom, to most of my desires." F. Scott Fitzgerald

***

"The things you hide in your heart—eat you alive."

***

"Did you know? It takes at least 6-8 months for the brain to process complete forgiveness, for someone who was hurt emotionally."

***

"One of the hardest lessons in life to learn is figuring out which bridges to cross and which to burn."

***

"Don't allow someone's misery to contaminate your happiness."

***

"Three ways to fail: first complain about everything, secondly blame others for your problems and finally never be grateful,"

***

"So I asked God, 'Why are you taking me through troubled waters?' He replied, 'Because your enemies can't swim."

***

"Grief is your true state of Liberty."

***

"One small crack does not mean that you are broken. It means that you were put to the test and didn't fall apart."

***

"If you hate a person then you are defeated by them."

***

"Worrying does not take away tomorrows troubles, it takes away todays peace."

***

"Never push a loyal person to the point where they walk away and no longer give a damn."

***

"We don't meet people by accident, they cross our paths for a reason."

***

"Real knowledge is to know the extent of one's ignorance."
Confucius

***

"Before you embark on a journey of revenge, dig two graves."
Confucius

***

"If it is still in your mind, it is still worth taking the risk."

***

"Love is serious mental illness." Plato

***

"You are good enough; you've just been giving yourself to the wrong people."

***

"In my life, I've lived, I've loved, I've lost, I've missed, I've hurt, I've trusted, I've made mistakes, but most of all I've learned—Shit Happens"

***

"The eyes tell more than words can ever say"

***

"Beautiful things happen in your life when you distance yourself from all the negative things."

***

"My head is saying, who cares about him, but my heart is screaming—I do"

***

"Sometimes people pretend you're a bad person so they don't feel guilty about the things they do to you."

***

"Poetry is when an emotion has found its thought, and the thought has found its words." Robert Frost

***

"It takes less time to do it right, then explain why you did it wrong." Longfellow

***

"The best way out is always through." Robert Frost

***

"I would rather be a beggar and be single, than be a Queen and married" Elizabeth I

***

"I die the king's good servant, but Gods First." St. Thomas More put to death for not joining the Church of England.

***

"Be very, very careful what you put into that head, because you will never, ever get it out." Thomas Cardinal Wolsey

***

"What peace can they have—if they are not at peace with GOD?" Matthew Henry

***

"My drops of tears I'll turn to sparks of fire," Shakespeare Henry VIII

***

"There shall be one mistress here and no master." Elizabeth I

***

"Though nothing can bring back the hour, or splendor in the grass, of glory in the flower; we will grieve not, rather find strength in what remains behind…" William Wordsworth

***

"The worst-tempered people I have ever met were those who
knew they were wrong." David Letterman

***

"I was better off healed than I ever was unbroken."

***

"I love the person I've become,
because I fought to become her."

***

"You're allowed to scream.
You're allowed to cry, but don't give up."

***

"Sometimes even normal feels wrong,"

***

"Extinguishing my candle doesn't make yours burn any
brighter."

***

"You'll never change your life
until you change your daily routine."

***

"You can't sell dreams to someone who is a nightmare."

***

"It's the quiet ones ya gotta watch."

***

"If you're not lighting any candles,
don't complain about being in the dark."

***

"One of the hardest things to do is letting go of what you
thought was forever."

***

"I was never sure if you were the darkness or the storm."

***

"I'm not the solution to your problems, I'm another problem."

***

"Why don't you take a nap, your face looks like a bag of
walnuts?"

***

"Perpetuating the lie, how do you sleep at night—
on a bed of money,"

***

"They can't do what we do and they hate us for it."

***

"We can solve this problem with a flask."

***

"I'm the master of my fate and the captain of my soul."

***

"Tell yourself the next one will be better, because it will."

***

"I guess what I'm saying is at some point,
we've all parked in the wrong garage."

***

"You're all so cynical, you don't smile, you smirk."

***

"Advertising is based on one thing, happiness."

***

"Because alcohol tastes better than tears,"

***

"A woman has to love a bad man once in a while to be thankful
for the good one" Elizabeth Taylor

***

"When people say 'She's got everything,'
I haven't got tomorrow." Liz Taylor

***

"Where your treasure is, your heart will be." Fr. Mark Dinardo

***

"He put me through hell
and I was the fool who called it LOVE"

***

"It's never too late to do the right thing,"

***

"The problem with people, who have no vices, is they are
pretty sure to have some annoying virtues."
(This is why I don't trust people who don't drink)

***

"No matter how you feel, get up, dress up,
show up and never give up."

***

"How do you explain war to a child? Furthermore why?"

***

"We've been invaded by the cellphone."

***

"Why is it when I get a pay raise, they raise prices?"

***

"It's never right to hit and run except in BASEBALL."

***

"Americans live to work, everyone else works to live."

***

"It's so over…there is no word for it."

***

"Stress would be more palatable—covered in chocolate."

***

"Revenge is a dish best served cold."

***

"Hell hath no worry as a woman scorned" Shakespeare

***

"In order to be scared, you must give into fear."

***

"Have a short memory when it comes to moving forward."

***

"Why is it so hard to let go of the past?"

***

"Jealously is a form of hatred."

***

"Respect is a one way street, don't expect it returned."

***

"Anything different is always something better."

***

"Definition of insanity is doing the same thing,
but expecting different results."

***

"Stop looking for happiness in the same place you lost it."

***

♫"Maybe I should have saved those left over dreams
Funny, but here's that rainy day
Here's that rainy day they told me about
And I laughed at the thought that it might turn out this way

Where is that worn out wish that I threw aside
After it brought my lover near
It's funny how love becomes a cold rainy day
Funny, that rainy day is here

Funny how love becomes a cold rainy day
Funny, that rainy day is here."♪

***

"Memories may be beautiful and yet what's too painful to remember, we simply choose to forget. So it's the laughter we will remember. Whenever we remember—the way we were."

***

"H.O.P.E –hold on pain ends"

***

"I just really, really, miss you and I quite don't know what to do about that."

***

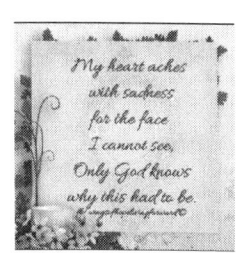

Chapter 24. Positive Thinking

Let's face it; successful people are very refine, happy and positive most of the time. Things can be difficult, things can get worse, but remaining optimistic will keep money in your purse. Positive thinking will keep you on track, even when you feel there are knives at your back.

****

"Teachers plant seeds in the minds of our future."

***

"You are far too smart
to be the only thing standing in your way"

***

"Success is achieved by development of our strengths,
not by elimination of our weakness."

***

"A river cuts through a rock not because of its power,
but its persistence."

***

"Get busy about being poor or be poor."

***

"What lies behind us and what lies before us are tiny compared to what lies within us."

***

"People mistake niceness for weakness."

***

"Without positive thinking for 7 days it makes one weak."

***

"Never underestimate anyone that's how you get beat."

***

"Confidence is the feeling you have before you know better."

***

"Minds are like parachutes—they only function when open."

***

"Your attitude is either the lock on, or the key to the door of success." Denis Waitley

***

"Your destiny has options."

***

"There's no mortgage on your life, you own it."

***

"If your actions inspire others to dream more, learn more, do more and become more, you are a leader." John Quincy Adams

***

"Rock bottom has built more champions
than privilege ever did."

***

"Open your arms to change, but don't let go of your values."
Dalai Lama

***

"Never let your fears decide your future." John Gotti

***

"Winners are not people who never fail,
but people who never quit."

***

"I don't want you to save me; I want you to stand by my side
as I save myself." John Gotti

***

"Success is not built on failure. It's built on frustration.
Sometimes it's built on Catastrophe."

***

"I hate when people ask me what I'll be doing in 2 years, come
on guys I don't have 2020 vision."

***

"Skills are cheap—passion is priceless."

***

"Going in one more round when you don't think you can—
that's what makes all the difference in your life." Rocky

***

"Stick to the things you really love. An honest room is always
up to date." Billy Baldwin

***

"Don't chase love, money or success. Become the best version
of yourself and those things will chase you."

***

"Screw-it—Let's do it!"

***

"Happiness keeps you SWEET. Trials keep you STRONG.
Sorrows keep you HUMAN. Failures keep you HUMBLE.
And God keeps you GOING."

***

"Success is not final, failure is not fatal; it is the courage to
continue that counts." Sir Winston Churchill

***

"The lesson is in the journey, the reward is the GOAL."

***

"Never chase what you want. Elevate your game until what
you want pursues you."

***

"Don't let other people tell you what you want" Pat Riley

***

"Never cut, when you can untie." Robert Frost

***

"You may see me struggle, but you'll never see me quit."

***

"Ability is what you're capable of doing, motivation
determines what you do
and attitude determines how well you do it."

***

"Veni, Vidi, Vici, I came, I saw, I conquered"

***

"Work hard in silence. Let success make your noise."

***

"Success is not built on success, it's built on failure. It's built
on frustration. Sometimes it built on catastrophe."

***

"I'm in charge of thinking of things
before people know they need them."

***

"Everything you can imagine is real." Pablo Picasso

***

"Follow your passion; follow your heart
and the things you need, will come."

***

"Dress SHABBY and they remember the dress, dress IMPECCABLY and they remember the woman." Coco Chanel

***

"Positive Mind, Positive Vibes, Positive Life."

***

"Live so that you can look any man in the eye and tell him to go to hell." Engineer working on the Panama Canal

***

"A messy desk is a sign of a dedicated employee."

***

"Don't be one of those here today gone tomorrow success stories."

***

"Attitude is everything."

***

"Are you sure you gave it your all?"

***

"Learn to read between the lines
and you'll make it in this world."

***

"My statute of limitations is running out."

***

"50% of something is better than100% of nothing"

***

"If you keep busy, you won't have time to get old."

***

"You really never get over it; you just find a way through it."

***

"We like the Job, the effort means more."

***

"Don't fuck with what's working."

***

"Fame and fortune are products of POSITVE THINKING."

***

"You've got WIT." (Whatever it takes)

***

"Being average is half way to being PERFECT."

***

"Good examples can overcome a lot of bad advice."

***

"If you can envision yourself succeeding, you'll get there."

***

"If you're going to play—play to win."

***

"In order to move forward, we must learn from our past."

***

"You'll never fail—unless you stop trying."

***

"Success is not easy, you have to work hard to get it
and ever harder to keep it."

***

"It's not worth winning if you don't have to fight for it."

***

"Love, hate and Passion always equal SUCCESS."

***

"Your faith can move mountains and your doubt can create
them."

***

"Create a life that feels good on the inside
not just looks good on the outside."

***

"Anything is possible is you've got enough nerve."

***

"Better to burn out—than fade away,"

***

"You are better to shoot for the moon and be among the stars, than shoot for fence and hit the dirt." URS

***

"What you lack in experience, make-up for in effort."

***

"Talent, drive and determination wins the game."

***

"It all begins and ends in your mind. What you give power to has power over you."

***

"I do have an unfair advantage over you, it don't quit—ever."

***

"Believe in yourself even when nobody else will."

***

"It's okay to live a life that others don't understand."

***

"90% of the work is done by 10% of the people."

***

"Make your parents proud, your enemies jealous and yourself happy."

***

"Failure should always be followed up by celebration. Otherwise you're not working hard enough."

***

"Work until you no longer need to introduce yourself."

***

"I'm just going to keep doing what I'm doing, keep proving people wrong and myself right."

***

"Don't give up! The beginning is always the hardest."

***

"If you want to go big, stop thinking small."

***

"Work until expensive becomes cheap."

***

"If you can't build with them, don't chill with them."

***

"Only lazy people have time to hate."

***

"Become so financially secure that you forget its PAYDAY."

***

Chapter 25. Humble

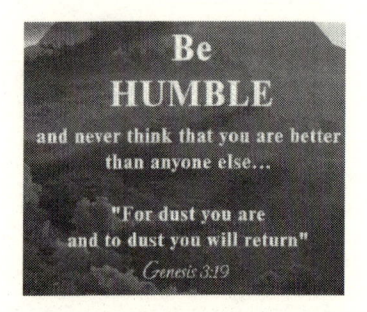

Humble by definition: Having or showing a modest or low estimate of one's own importance.

A person of faith is humble of course; they're kind and honest without any remorse. Humble people are successful, tried and true; they're willing to help, in all that you do. Most make you smile and can chase away doom; they emanate kindness, just by entering a room.

****

"If I'm an advocate for anything, it's to move. As far as you can, as much as you can. Across the ocean, or simply across the river, walk in someone else's shoes or at least eat their food. It's a plus for everyone." Anthony Bourdain (Suicide 6/2018)

***

"All I want to do is go the distance." Rocky

***

"Respond intelligently even to unintelligent treatment."

***

"Silence is often misinterpreted, but never misquoted."

***

"Age plus time equals experience and know how."

***

"The winter blahs melt into spring."

***

"To be humble is to be honest with yourself,"

***

"Kindness is the oil that takes friction out of life."

***

"A house divided against its self—can't stand."

***

"If you hate something—you must have liked it first."

***

"You can get people to conform if you guide instead of push."

***

"There's more to being the best than just winning."

***

"A fan is good when the heat is on and when you're feeling low."

***

"Laugh every day it's like inner jogging."

***

"Be careful of the words you speak. Make them soft and sweet;
you'll never know from day to day
which ones you'll have to eat."

***

"If we forget our troubles as readily as we forget our blessings,
we'd have peace on earth."

***

"To belittle is to be little."

***

"Whatever makes you feel the sun from the inside out—
chase that,"

***

"Every champion was once a contender
that refused to give up."

***

"Whoever is trying to bring you down is already below you."

***

"Even a broken clock is right twice a day."

***

"If you don't sacrifice for what you want, what you want
becomes the sacrifice."

***

"Wisdom—is the ability to be kind in unkind circumstances."
Dr. Shawne.com

***

"It takes a lot of courage to show your dreams to someone
else." Erma Bombeck

***

"Our greatest glory is not in falling,
but in the rising every time we fall." Rocky Balboa

***

"Expect nothing—appreciate everything."

***

"The life in front of you is far more important
than the life behind you."

***

"Hate is heavy—let it go."

***

"I didn't change, I just woke up." Sandeep Kumar

***

"Whatever happens, wherever you go, whatever you do,
remember this; no one can take the fire in your soul, the stars
from your eyes, the passion in your heart. Those are yours
forever." SLAL

***

"The sign of intelligence is that you are constantly wondering. Idiots are always dead-sure about every damn thing they are doing in their life." Vasudev

***

"Just a man and his will to survive." Rocky

***

"All those fights, you beat'em with HEART—not muscle," Adrienne Balboa

***

"Kids keep you young, informed and broke."

***

"Judge your success by what you had to give up, to get it."

***

"My favorite place is inside your hugs."

***

"Better a diamond with a flaw then a pebble."

***

"If you want to feel rich—just count all the things you have that money can't buy."

***

"Peace, Love and Joy, three little words to get you through the day."

***

"Humility is the solid foundation for all virtues." Confucius

***

"Gratitude is the fairest blossom which springs from the soul."
Henry Ward Beecher

***

"Be humble and never think you are better than anyone else—
for dust you are and to dust you will return." Genesis 3:19

***

"You can be quiet and reserved and still be witty and even
outgoing in certain circles."

***

"You can be intelligent and sharp-minded
and still forget what month it is."

***

"If you are the smartest person in the room, you are in the
wrong room."

***

"There are so many beautiful reasons to be happy."

***

"Be humble, be simple, and bring joy to others." St Madeleine
Sophie Barat

***

"Everything will be alright in the end,
if it's not, then it's not the end yet."

***

"Keep Calm and stay classy."

***

"Fashion changes, but style endures."

***

"Always dress well, but keep it simple."

***

"Nothing beautiful asks for attention."

***

"Never do the envy, jealously or insecure stuff, be the hustle, the well-wisher and the go-getter."

***

"Beauty begins the moment you decide to become yourself."

***

"Classy is when a woman has everything to flaunt, but chooses not to show it."

***

"Some people think Luxury is the opposite of poverty; it is not—it's the opposite of vulgarity."

***

"I love Luxury. And Luxury lies not in richness and ordination, but in the absence of vulgarity." Coco Chanel

***

"Fashion fades, only style remains the same." Coco Chanel

***

"Peace begins with a smile."

***

"I thank God for always giving me another chance."

***

"Everybody wants to belong."

***

"It will cost you more to say NO, than to say YES."

***

"If you don't risk a little you won't go anywhere."

***

"Your heart is a place to draw true happiness,"

***

"He who knows he has enough is rich."

***

"Your problem is not inability, but inconsistency."

***

"You see a problem, I see potential."

***

"Remember the little people on your way up, you're bound to see them on your way down."

***

"If there were no critics, who would keep us reaching, improving and surpassing?"

***

"The problems with today—we use people and value things."

***

"My job is to see past the bullshit."

***

"Don't mix imagination with fear."

***

"Don't sulk; it's a sign of weakness."

***

"Becoming number one is easier than remaining number one."

***

"The trouble with happiness—you can't buy it."

***

"Real love is helping someone who can never return the favor."

***

"Live that when death comes, the mourners outnumber the cheering section."

***

"The proper time to do the proper thing is before you have to do it."

***

"The best way to get even is to forget."

***

"Find what works for you and stick with it."

***

"The first step toward gaining eternal life
is admitting we don't deserve it."

***

"Time is for the taking, don't miss your share."

***

"Working at perfection is never wasted time."

***

"The best THINGS in life are not THINGS."

***

"Handling diversity well is the source of your strength."

***

"Failure doesn't mean you'll not succeed;
it will just take a bit more effort."

***

"Seas the day."

***

"Even a brick aspires to be something."

***

"Dear God I have a problem…it's me."

***

"It takes time to build up confidence
and no time to knock it down."

***

"It all started with a penny."

***

"Would you rather be feared, or loved?"

***

"One who has class need never to remind others?"

***

"Always be thankful for the bad things in life. They open your
eyes to see the good things you weren't paying attention to
before."

***

"Save money and money will save you."

***

"If you are helping someone and expecting something in
return, you are doing business not KINDNESS."

***

"Dust off your courage and find your fire."

***

"When nails grow long, we cut nails not fingers. Similarly when misunderstandings grow up, cut your ego, not your relationship."

***

"I don't know the key to success, but the key to failure is trying to please everyone."

***

"For every minute you are angry you lose sixty seconds of happiness."

***

"On a clear day how it will astound you that the glow of your being outshines every star"

***

"All of us have special ones who have loved us into being."

***

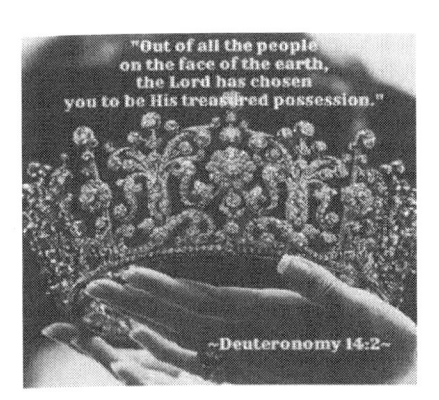

Chapter26.The Final Word

In the end will you be remembered in all that you do, will your legacy be grand and full of virtue? Will your words be your legacy or just a fable, written on the wall, or left on the table? God's only wish is that we help one another out. It's ashamed we're all going through a selfless drought. I believe we are here to do all we can, to find our God given talent, just like BATMAN. Love one another in all that you do, these are Gods words, for me and for you. Make room for God in your life and in your heart—remember my friends, it's never too late to start.

****

"Nothing is impossible; the word itself says it—I'M Possible."

***

"Candy makes life a bit sweeter."

***

"Roads were made for Journey's not destinations." Confucius

***

"Say yes, you'll figure it out afterwards."

***

"The man on the mountain never fell there." Vince Lombardi

***

"I can. I will. End of story."

***

"Presidential politics every 4 years—different players same old game,"

***

"If you ever stop working—you'll rust."

***

"Practice hard, you'll play the way you practiced."

***

"Do what you have to do first and what you want second."

***

"The only place success comes before work is in the dictionary."

***

"Real success is not on the stage, but off the stage as a human being and how you get along with your fellow man."
Sammy Davis Jr. RIP 5/16/1990

***

"Inspiration + perspiration = graduation."

***

"Watch who you trust, even your teeth bite your tongue every once in a while."

***

"Those who want respect, give respect."
Tony Soprano RIP2013

***

"I've failed over and over again in my life
and that is why I succeed." Michael Jordan

***

"Everybody loves you until you become competition."

***

"Edward J. Smith, the captain of TITANIC, said his last words
to the crew: 'Well boys, do your best for the women and
children, and look out for yourself." Sinking 4/1912

***

"I respect those who tell me the truth,
no matter how hard it is." Michael Corleone

***

"Trust me, when you mind your own business,
life is way less stressful."

***

"Be fascinating to someone,"

***

"If life just got a little bit harder,
it probably means you just leveled up."

***

"People hate you for one of these reasons: 1.They hate themselves. 2. They want to be you. 3. They see you as a threat."

***

"Success is a lousy teacher. It seduces smart people into thinking they can't lose." Bill Gates

***

"We are all one bad decision away from devastation."

***

"I am an acquired taste. Don't like me? Acquire some taste."

***

"Be around those who feed your soul, not eat it."

***

"The man who moves a mountain—begins by carrying away small stones." Confucius

***

"Nobody is gonna hit as hard as life, but it ain't how hard you can hit. It's how hard you can get hit and keep moving forward. It's how much you can take, and keep moving forward—that's how winning is done." Sylvester Stallone (Rocky)

***

"Unless I can learn from you, I don't have time for you."

***

"The two most important days in your life are the day you were born, and the day you find out why." Mark Twain

***

"Let go of people who dull your shine, poison your spirit, and bring you drama. Cancel your subscriptions to their issues."

***

WAKE THE FUCK UP
"Sleep early, prepare your meals in advance, kill your workouts, stop making excuses, do your job like a boss, make your friends laugh, love your family, stop being a drama queen and wake the fuck up." The Lacey Credo

***

"Kindness is the language which the deaf can hear and the blind can see." Mark Twain

***

"The truth is that if Israel were to put down its arms there would be no more Israel. If the Arabs were to put down their arms there would be no more war." Benjamin Netanyahu

***

"I don't stop when I'm tired—I stop when I'm done." James Bond.

***

"Meraki: (v) to do something with soul, creativity, or love; to put something of yourself into your work."

***

"The meaning of life is to find your gift. The purpose of life is to give it away." William Shakespeare

***

"Tell people what they want to hear, you can sell them anything." A concierge

***

"When you love what you do—you can't be away from it for too long" Wendy Williams

***

"Happiness is an inside job; don't give anyone that much power."

***

"Don't wish for it, work for it."

***

"Sometimes a thing worth doing is worth overdoing." David Letterman.

***

"Everything you want is on the other side of fear."

***

"Doubt kills more dreams than failure ever will"

***

"Go out and buy yourself a 5 cent pencil and a 10 cent notebook and begin to write down some million-dollar ideas for yourself."

***

"Success is not final, failure is not fatal, it is the courage to continue that counts" Winston Churchill

***

"Motivation is what gets your started; habit is what keeps it going."

***

"Your life is your message to the world, make sure it's inspiring."

***

"In the end, we all just want someone that chooses us—over everyone else, under any circumstances."

***

"The riches people in the world look for and build networks. Everyone else looks for work."

***

"Work until your signature becomes an autograph."

***

"SUCCESS depends on the second letter."

***

"Marketing is transferring enthusiasm to the customer."

***

"In order to be IRREPLACELABLE, one must always be DIFFERENT." Coco Chanel

***

"I have one life and it only goes in one direction, forward."

***

"A goal should scare you a little and excite you a lot." sylvia

***

"ADORNMENT, what a science! BEAUTY what a weapon!

MODESTY, what ELLEGANCE."

***

"You don't have to be rich to sparkle."

***

"A grateful heart is a magnet for miracles."

***

"I don't know how my story will end, but nowhere is my text will it ever read...I gave up."

***

"Tell me I won't and I might, tell me I can't and I will."

***

"It's not the having, it's the getting."

***

"I never face the day without perfume."

***

"Jewelry has the power to be that one little thing that makes you feel unique."

***

"Eat DIAMONDS for breakfast and shine all day."

***

"In a world full of trends, I'm going to remain a CLASSC."

***

"Confusion is a state of being, some never recover."

***

"A mother like no other,"

***

"A chain is only as strong as its weakest link."

***

"What good are rules if you can't break them?"

***

"If the best is yet to come—it better hurry up."

***

"I've been stabbed in the back by those I needed the most. I've been lied to by those I love, and I have felt alone when I couldn't afford to be, but at the end of the day I had to learn to be my own best friend, because there is going to be days when no-one is going to be there for me, but myself."

***

"Trust no one."

***

"Eagles we are not, but we can still fly."

***

"Let your imagination be your wings."

***

"It's us against them."

***

"Extreme in any direction is bad."

***

"If it feels good, do it."

***

"Never drive faster than your guardian angel can fly."

***

"The tassel is worth the hassle."

***

"Don't bite the hand that feeds you."

***

"The meaning of success—knowing when you've reached it,"

***

"Don't make your life a solo mission."

***

"Nepotism does not make good business cents."

***

"Stop with all those excuses."

***

"People spend money on things they don't need, to impress people they don't even like."

***

"It was fun while it lasted"

***

"You never know what you got until it's gone."

***

"Where would you be without ambition?"

***

"Opera touches the soul and stays there till you die."

***

"You can't hit the ball unless you take a swing."

***

"What we need today is not a NEW DEAL, SQUARE DEAL or FAIR DEAL, but just IDEALS."

***

"When all is said and done, will you be satisfied?"

***

"When you mix business with pleasure, you are asking for trouble." mom

***

"A Father is someone you look up to no matter how tall you get."

***

"If you're too open-minded your brains will fall out."

***

"My parents gave me life and later gave me words to live by."

***

"My family has blessed me with comfort, self-worth and a rich history."

***

"Age is a high-price to pay for maturity."

***

"My greatest fear in life is not to be challenged."

***

"My best work is still ahead of me."

***

"Every one of us is called to minister."

***

"We are living stones, build a castle."

***

"Just because you're aging doesn't mean you're old."

***

"It's hard to steer a parked car."

***

"One way to get people to slow down—call it work"

***

"Go in Peace my Friends."

***

"Goest & Fucketh Thyself."

***

DO ~~NT~~

~~QU~~ IT

Sandeep Kumar

***

"There is no possibility of success without Risk."

***

"Be the one who gave a damn."

***

"Learn all you can, you can face anything."

***

Drive Expensive
Wear Italian
Drink Russian
Kiss French
Be happy

***

"I hope to arrive to my death, late, in love, and a little drunk."

***

7 Rules of Life

*Make peace with your past so it won't disturb your future.

*What other people think of you is none of your business.

*The only person in charge of your happiness is you.

*Don't compare your life to others. Comparison is the thief of joy.

*Time heals almost everything. Give it time.

*STOP thinking so much. It's alright not to know all the answers.

*SMILE you don't own all the problems of the world

***

"When it comes to dreams—think BIG."

***

"Like a Rose under the April snow…"

***

"Stay true to yourself—people respond to authenticity."

***

"Discovering the truth about ourselves is a lifetime's work, but it's worth the effort." Mister Rogers

***

"In the end we all become stories."

***

"In the end you tried, you cared and sometimes that is enough."

***

I leave you with my last Quote

A sincere and proper antidote;

Work with your friends

Dine with family

And pray for tomorrow…

Sylvia Louise Alexandria Lacey

Notable

Quotable

A Gemstone Novel

June 2018

Notable Quotable

By

Sylvia Louise Alexandria Lacey

Left Blank for you to jot down your quotes…

Left Blank for you to jot down your quotes…

Left Blank for you to jot down your quotes…

Notable Quotable

A Gemstone Novel

June 2018

Notable Quotable

By

Sylvia Louise Alexandria Lacey

Made in the USA
Columbia, SC
24 June 2018